TATTI

THE STORY OF A STREET ARAB.

BY
HORATIO ALGER, Jr.

To
AMOS AND O. AUGUSTA CHENEY,
This Volume
IS DEDICATED
BY THEIR AFFECTIONATE BROTHER.

PREFACE.

When, three years since, the author published "Ragged Dick," he was far from anticipating the flattering welcome it would receive, or the degree of interest which would be excited by his pictures of street life in New York. The six volumes which comprised his original design are completed, but the subject is not exhausted. There are yet other phases of street life to be described, and other classes of street Arabs, whose fortunes deserve to be chronicled.

"Tattered Tom" is therefore presented to the public as the initial volume of a new series of six stories, which may be regarded as a continuation of the "Ragged Dick Series." Some surprise may be felt at the discovery that Tom is a girl; but I beg to assure my readers that she is not viiione of the conventional kind. Though not without her good points, she will be found to differ very widely in tastes and manners from the young ladies of twelve usually to be met in society. I venture to hope that she will become a favorite in spite of her numerous faults, and that no less interest will be felt in her fortunes than in those of the heroes of earlier volumes.

TATTERED TOM;
OR,
THE ADVENTURES OF A STREET ARAB.
CHAPTER I.
INTRODUCES TATTERED TOM.

Mr. Frederic Pelham, a young gentleman very daintily dressed, with exquisitely fitting kids and highly polished boots, stood at the corner of Broadway and Chambers Streets, surveying with some dismay the dirty crossing, and speculating as to his chances of getting over without marring the polish of his boots.

He started at length, and had taken two steps, when a dirty hand was thrust out, and he was saluted by the request, "Gi' me a penny, sir?"

"Out of my way, you bundle of rags!" he answered.

"You're another!" was the prompt reply.

Frederic Pelham stared at the creature who had dared to imply that he—a leader of fashion—was a bundle of rags.

The street-sweeper was apparently about twelve years of age. It was not quite easy to determine whether it was a boy or girl. The head was surmounted by a boy's cap, the hair was cut short, it wore a boy's jacket, but underneath was a girl's dress. Jacket and dress were both in a state of extreme raggedness. The child's face was very dark and, as might be expected, dirty; but it was redeemed by a pair of brilliant black eyes, which were fixed upon the young exquisite in an expression half-humorous, half-defiant, as the owner promptly retorted, "You're another!"

"Clear out, you little nuisance!" said the dandy, stopping short from necessity, for the little sweep had planted herself directly in his path; and to step out on either side would have soiled his boots irretrievably.

"Gi' me a penny, then?"

"I'll hand you to the police, you little wretch!"

"I aint done nothin'. Gi' me a penny?"

Mr. Pelham, provoked, raised his cane threateningly.

But Tom (for, in spite of her being a girl, this was the name by which she was universally known; indeed she scarcely knew any other) was wary. She dodged the blow, and by an adroit sweep of her broom managed to scatter some mud on Mr. Pelham's boots.

"You little brat, you've muddied my boots!" he exclaimed, with vexation.

"Then why did you go for to strike me?" said Tom, defiantly.

He did not stop to answer, but hurried across the street. His pace was accelerated by an approaching vehicle, and the instinct of self-preservation, more powerful than even the dictates of fashion, compelled him to make a détour through the mud, greatly to the injury of his no longer immaculate boots. But there was a remedy for the disaster on the other side.

"Shine your boots, sir?" asked a boot-black, who had stationed himself at the other side of the crossing.

Frederic Pelham looked at his boots. Their glory had departed. Their virgin gloss had been dimmed by plebeian mud. He grudged the boot-black's fee, for he was thoroughly mean, though he had plenty of money at his command. But it was impossible to walk up Broadway in such boots. Suppose he should meet any of his fashionable friends, especially if ladies, his fashionable reputation would be endangered.

"Go ahead, boy!" he said. "Do your best."

"All right, sir."

"It's the second time I've had my boots blacked this morning. If it hadn't been for that dirty sweep I should have got across safely."

The boy laughed—to himself. He knew Tom well enough, and he had been an interested spectator of her encounter with his present customer, having an eye to business. But he didn't think it prudent to make known his thoughts.

The boots were at length polished, and Mr. Pelham saw with satisfaction that no signs of the street mire remained.

"How much do you want, boy?" he asked.

"Ten cents."

"I thought five cents was the price."

"Can't afford to work on no such terms."

Mr. Pelham might have disputed the fee, but he saw an acquaintance approaching, and did not care to be caught chaffering with a boot-black. He therefore reluctantly drew out a dime, and handed it to the boy, who at once deposited it in the pocket of a ragged vest.

He stood on the sidewalk on the lookout for another customer, when Tom marched across the street, broom in hand.

"I say, Joe, how much did he give you?"

"Ten cents."

"How much yer goin' to give me?"

"Nothin'!"

"You wouldn't have got him if I hadn't muddied his boots."

"Did you do it a-purpose?"

Tom nodded.

"What for?"

"He called me names. That's one reason. Besides, I wanted to give you a job."

Joe seemed struck by this view, and, being alive to his own interest, did not disregard the application.

"Here's a penny," he said.

"Gi' me two."

He hesitated a moment, then diving once more into his pocket, brought up another penny, which Tom transferred with satisfaction to the pocket of her dress.

"Shall I do it ag'in?" she asked.

"Yes," said Joe. "I say, Tom, you're a smart un."

"I'd ought to be. Granny makes me smart whenever she gets a chance."

Tom returned to the other end of the crossing, and began to sweep diligently. Her labors did not extend far from the curbstone, as the stream of vehicles now rapidly passing would have made it dangerous. However, it was all one to Tom where she swept. The cleanness of the crossing was to her a matter of comparative indifference. Indeed, considering her own disregard of neatness, it could hardly have been expected that she should feel very solicitous on that point. Like some of her elders who were engaged in municipal labors, she regarded street-sweeping as a "job," out of which she was to make money, and her interest began and ended with the money she earned.

There were not so many to cross Broadway at this point as lower down, and only a few of these seemed impressed by a sense of the pecuniary value of Tom's services.

"Gi' me a penny, sir," she said to a stout gentleman.

He tossed a coin into the mud.

Tom darted upon it, and fished it up, wiping her fingers afterwards upon her dress.

"Aint you afraid of soiling your dress?" asked the philanthropist, smiling.

"What's the odds?" said Tom, coolly.

"You're a philosopher," said the stout gentleman.

"Don't you go to callin' me names!" said Tom; "'cause if you do I'll muddy up your boots."

"So you don't want to be called a philosopher?" said the gentleman.

"No, I don't," said Tom, eying him suspiciously.

"Then I must make amends."

He took a dime from his pocket, and handed it to the astonished Tom.

"Is this for me?" she asked.

"Yes."

Tom's eyes glistened; for ten cents was a nugget when compared with her usual penny receipts. She stood in a brown study till her patron was half across the street, then, seized with a sudden idea, she darted after him, and tugged at his coat-tail.

"What's wanted?" he asked, turning round in some surprise.

"I say," said Tom, "you may call me that name ag'in for five cents more."

The ludicrous character of the proposal struck him, and he laughed with amusement.

"Well," he said, "that's a good offer. What's your name?"

"Tom."

"Which are you,—a boy or a girl?"

"I'm a girl, but I wish I was a boy."

"What for?"

"'Cause boys are stronger than girls, and can fight better."

"Do you ever fight?"

"Sometimes."

"Whom do you fight with?"

"Sometimes I fight with the boys, and sometimes with granny."

"What makes you fight with your granny?"

"She gets drunk and fires things at my head; then I pitch into her."

The cool, matter-of-fact manner in which Tom spoke seemed to amuse her questioner.

"I was right," he said; "you're a philosopher,—a practical philosopher."

"That's more'n you said before," said Tom; "I want ten cents for that."

The ten cents were produced. Tom pocketed them in a business-like manner, and went back to her employment. She wondered, slightly, whether a philosopher was something very bad; but, as there was no means of determining, sensibly dismissed the inquiry, and kept on with her work.

CHAPTER II
TOM GETS A SQUARE MEAL.

About twelve o'clock Tom began to feel the pangs of hunger. The exercise which she had taken, together with the fresh air, had stimulated her appetite. It was about the time when she was expected to go home, and accordingly she thrust her hand into her pocket, and proceeded to count the money she had received.

"Forty-two cents!" she said, at last, in a tone of satisfaction. "I don't generally get more'n twenty. I wish that man would come round and call me names every day."

Tom knew that she was expected to go home and carry the result of her morning's work to her granny; but the unusual amount suggested to her another idea. Her mid-day meal was usually of the plainest and scantiest,—a crust of dry bread, or a cold sausage on days of plenty,—and Tom sometimes did long for something better. But generally it would have been dangerous to appropriate a sufficient sum from her receipts, as the deficit would have been discovered, and quick retribution would have followed from her incensed granny, who was a vicious old woman with a pretty vigorous arm. Now, however, she could appropriate twenty cents without danger of discovery.

"I can get a square meal for twenty cents," Tom reflected, "and I'll do it."

But she must go home first, as delay would be dangerous, and have disagreeable consequences.

She prepared for the visit by dividing her morning's receipts into two parcels. The two ten-cent scrips she hid away in the lining of her tattered jacket. The pennies, including one five-cent scrip, she put in the pocket of her dress. This last was intended for her granny. She then started homewards, dragging her broom after her.

She walked to Centre Street, turned after a while into Leonard, and went on, turning once or twice, until she came to one of the most wretched tenement houses to be found in that not very choice locality. She passed through an archway leading into an inner court, on which fronted a rear house more shabby, if possible, than the front dwelling. The court was redolent of odors far from savory; children pallid, dirty, and unhealthy-looking, were playing about, filling the air with shrill cries, mingled with profanity; clothes were hanging from some of the windows; miserable and besotted faces were seen at others.

Tom looked up to a window in the fourth story. She could descry a woman, with a pipe in her mouth.

"Granny's home," she said to herself.

She went up three flights, and, turning at the top, went to the door and opened it.

It was a wretched room, containing two chairs and a table, nothing more. On one of the chairs was seated a large woman, of about sixty, with a clay pipe in her mouth. The room was redolent of the vilest tobacco-smoke.

This was granny.

If granny had ever been beautiful, there were no traces of that dangerous gift in the mottled and wrinkled face, with bleared eyes, which turned towards the door as Tom entered.

"Why didn't you come afore, Tom?" she demanded.

"I'm on time," said Tom. "Clock aint but just struck."

"How much have you got?"

Tom pulled out her stock of pennies and placed them in the woman's outstretched palm.

"There's twenty-two," she said.

"Umph!" said granny. "Where's the rest?"

"That's all."

"Come here."

Tom advanced, not reluctantly, for she felt sure that granny would not think of searching her jacket, especially as she had brought home as much as usual.

The old woman thrust her hand into the child's pocket, and turned it inside-out with her claw-like fingers, but not another penny was to be found.

"Umph!" she grunted, apparently satisfied with her scrutiny.

"Didn't I tell you so?" said Tom.

Granny rose from her chair, and going to a shelf took down a piece of bread, which had become dry and hard.

"There's your dinner," said she.

"Gi' me a penny to buy an apple," said Tom,—rather by way of keeping up appearances than because she wanted one. Visions of a more satisfactory repast filled her imagination.

"You don't want no apple. Bread's enough," said granny.

Tom was not much disappointed. She knew pretty well beforehand how her application would fare. Frequently she made sure of success by buying the apple and eating it before handing the proceeds of her morning's work to the old woman. To-day she had other views, which she was in a hurry to carry out.

She took the bread, and ate a mouthful. Then she slipped it into her pocket, and said, "I'll eat it as I go along, granny."

To this the old woman made no objection, and Tom went out.

In the court-yard below she took out her crust, and handed it to a hungry-looking boy of ten, the unlucky offspring of drunken parents, who oftentimes was unable to command even such fare as Tom obtained.

"Here, Tim," she said, "eat that; I aint hungry."

It was one of Tim's frequent fast days, and even the hard crust was acceptable to him. He took it readily, and began to eat it ravenously. Tom looked on with benevolent interest, feeling the satisfaction of having done a charitable act. The satisfaction might have been heightened by the thought that she was going to get something better herself.

"So you're hungry, Tim," she said.

"I'm always hungry," said Tim.

"Did you have any breakfast?"

"Only an apple I picked up in the street."

"He's worse off than me," thought Tom; but she had no time to reflect on the superior privileges of her own position, for she was beginning to feel hungry herself.

There was a cheap restaurant near by, only a few blocks away.

Tom knew it well, for she had often paused before the door and inhaled enviously the appetizing odor of the dishes which were there vended to patrons not over-fastidious, at prices accommodated to scantily lined pocket-books. Tom had never entered, but had been compelled to remain outside, wishing that a more propitious fortune had placed it in her power to dine there every day. Now, however, first thrusting her fingers into the lining of her jacket to make sure that the money was there, she boldly entered the restaurant and took a seat at one of the tables.

The room was not large, there being only eight tables, each of which might accommodate four persons. The floor was sanded, the tables were some of them bare, others covered with old newspapers, which had become greasy, and were rather worse than no table-cloth at all. The guests, of whom perhaps a dozen were seated at the table, were undoubtedly plebeian. Men in shirt-sleeves, rough-bearded sailors and 'long-shore men, composed the company, with one ragged boot-black, who had his blacking-box on the seat beside him.

It was an acquaintance of Tom, and she went and sat beside him.

"Do you get dinner here, Jim?" she asked.

"Yes, Tom; what brings you here?"

"I'm hungry."

"Don't you live along of your granny?"

"Yes; but I thought I'd come here to-day. What have you got?"

"Roast beef."

"Is it good?"

"Bully!"

"I'll have some, then. How much is it?"

"Ten cents."

Ten cents was the standard price in this economical restaurant for a plate of meat of whatever kind. Perhaps, considering the quality and amount given, it could not be regarded as very cheap; still the sum was small, and came within Tom's means.

A plate of beef was brought and placed before Tom. Her eyes dilated with pleasure as they rested on the delicious morsel. There was a potato besides; and a triangular slice of bread, with an infinitesimal dab of butter,—all for ten cents. But Tom's ambition soared higher.

"Bring me a cup o' coffee," she said to the waiter.

It was brought,—a very dark, muddy, suspicious-looking beverage,—a base libel upon the fragrant berry whose name it took; but such a thought did not disturb Tom. She never doubted that it was what it purported to be. She stirred it vigorously with the spoon, and sipped it as if it had been nectar.

"Aint it prime just?" she exclaimed, smacking her lips.

Then ensued a vigorous onslaught upon the roast beef. It was the first meat Tom had tasted for weeks, with the exception of occasional cold sausage; and she was in the seventh heaven of delight as she hurriedly ate it. When she had finished, the plate was literally and entirely empty. Tom did not believe in leaving anything behind. She was almost tempted to "lick the platter clean," but observed that none of the other guests did so, and refrained.

"Bring me a piece of apple pie," said Tom, determined for once to have what she denominated a "good square meal." The price of the pie being five cents, this would just exhaust her funds. Payment was demanded when the pie was brought, the prudent waiter having some fears that his customer was eating beyond her means.

Tom paid the money, and, vigorously attacking the pie, had almost finished it, when, chancing to lift her eyes to the window, she saw a sight that made her blood curdle.

Looking through the pane with a stony glare that meant mischief was her granny, whom she had supposed safe at home.

CHAPTER III
CAUGHT IN THE ACT.
It was Tom's ill luck that brought granny upon the scene, contrary to every reasonable expectation. After smoking out her pipe, she made up her mind to try another smoke, when she found that her stock of tobacco was exhausted. Being constitutionally lazy, it was some minutes before she made up her mind to go out and lay in a fresh supply. Finally she decided, and made her way downstairs to the court, and thence to the street.

Tim saw her, and volunteered the information, "Tom gave me some bread."

"When?" demanded granny.

"When she come out just now."

"What did she do that for?"

"She said she wasn't hungry."

The old woman was puzzled. Tom's appetite was usually quite equal to the supply of food which she got. Could Tom have secreted some money to buy apples? This was hardly likely, since she had carefully searched her. Besides, Tom had returned the usual amount. Still, granny's suspicions were awakened, and she determined to question Tom when she returned at the close of the afternoon.

The tobacco shop where granny obtained her tobacco was two doors beyond the restaurant where Tom was then enjoying her cheap dinner with a zest which the guests at Delmonico's do not often bring to the discussion of their more aristocratic viands. It was only a chance that led granny, as she passed, to look in; but that glance took in all who were seated at the tables, including Tom.

Had granny received an invitation to preside at a meeting in the Cooper Institute, she would hardly have been more surprised than at the sight of Tom, perfidiously enjoying a meal out of money from which she had doubtless been defrauded.

"The owdacious young reprobate!" muttered the old woman, glaring fiercely at her unconscious victim.

But Tom just then happened to look up, as we have seen. Her heart gave a sudden thump, and she said to herself, "I'm in for a lickin', that's so. Granny's mad as blazes."

The old woman did not long leave her in doubt as to the state of her feelings.

She strode into the eating-house, and, advancing to the table, seized Tom by the arm.

"What are you here for?" she growled, in a hoarse voice.

"To get some dinner," said Tom.

By this time she had recovered from her temporary panic. She had courage and pluck, and was toughened by the hard life she had led into a stoical endurance of the evils from which she could not escape.

"What business had you to come?"

"I was hungry."

"Didn't I give you a piece of bread?"

"I didn't like it."

"What did you buy?"

"A plate of beef, a cup o' coffee, and some pie. Better buy some, granny. They're bully."

"You're a reg'lar bad un. You'll fetch up on the gallus," said granny, provoked at Tom's coolness.

So saying, she seized Tom by the shoulder roughly. But by this time the keeper of the restaurant thought fit to interfere.

"We can't have any disturbance here, ma'am," he said. "You must leave the room."

"She had no right to get dinner here," said granny. "I won't let her pay for it."

"She has paid for it already."

"Is that so?" demanded the old woman, disappointed.

Tom nodded, glad to have outwitted her guardian.

"It was my money. You stole it."

"No it wa'n't. A gentleman give it to me for callin' me names."

"Come out of here!" said granny, jerking Tom from her chair. "Don't you let her have no more to eat here," she added, turning to the keeper of the restaurant.

"She can eat here whenever she's got money to pay for it."

Rather disgusted at her failure to impress the keeper of the restaurant with her views in the matter, granny emerged into the street with Tom in her clutches.

She gave her a vigorous shaking up on the sidewalk.

"How do you like that?" she demanded.

"I wish I was as big as you!" said Tom, indignantly.

"Well, what if you was?" demanded the old woman, pausing in her punishment, and glaring at Tom.

"I'd make your nose bleed," said Tom, doubling up her fist.

"You would, would you?" said granny, fiercely. "Then it's lucky you aint;" and she gave her another shake.

"Where are you going to take me?" asked Tom.

"Home. I'll lock you up for a week, and give you nothin' to eat but bread once a day."

"All right!" said Tom. "If I'm locked up at home, I can't bring you any money."

This consideration had not at first suggested itself to the vindictive old woman. It would cut off all her revenue to punish Tom as she proposed; and this would be far from convenient. But anger was more powerful just then than policy; and she determined at all events to convey Tom home, and give her a flogging, before sending her out into the street to resume her labors.

She strode along, dragging Tom by the arm; and not another word was spoken till they reached the rear tenement house.

"What's the matter with the child?" asked Mrs. Murphy, who had just come down into the court after one of her own children.

"She stole my money," said granny; "and was eatin' a mighty fine dinner out of it."

"It was my money, Mrs. Murphy," said Tom. "I gave granny twenty-two cents when I came home."

"I hope you won't go to hurt the child," said kind-hearted Mrs. Murphy.

"I'll be much obliged to you, Mrs. Murphy, if you'll mind your own business," said granny, loftily. "When I want your advice, mum, I'll come and ask it; begging your pardon, mum."

"She's a tough craythur," said Mrs. Murphy to herself. "She beats that poor child too bad entirely."

Granny drew Tom into the room with no gentle hand.

"Now you're goin' to catch it," said she, grimly.

Tom was of the same opinion, and meant to defend herself as well as she knew how. She had all her wits about her, and had already planned out her campaign.

On the chair was a stout stick which granny was accustomed to use on such occasions as the present. When wielded by a vigorous arm, it was capable of inflicting considerable pain, as Tom very well knew. That stick she determined to have.

Accordingly when granny temporarily released her hold of her, as she entered the room, Tom sprang for the chair, seized the stick, and sent it flying out of the window.

"What did you do that for?" said granny, fiercely.

"I don't want to be licked," said Tom, briefly.

"You're going to be, then."

"Not with the stick."

"We'll see."

Granny poked her head out of the window, and saw Tim down in the court.

"Bring up that stick," she said; "that's a good boy."

Tim picked up the stick, and was about to obey the old woman's request, when he heard another voice—Tom's—from the other window.

"Don't you do it, Tim. Granny wants to lick me."

That was enough. Tim didn't like the old woman,—no one in the building did,—and he did like Tom, who, in spite of being a tough customer, was good-natured and obliging, unless her temper was aroused by the old woman's oppression. So Tim dropped the stick.

"Bring it right up," said granny, angrily.

"Are you goin' to lick Tom?"

"None of your business! Bring it up, or I'll lick you too."

"No, you don't!" answered Tim. "You must come for it yourself if you want it."

Granny began to find that she must do her own errands. It was an undertaking to go down three flights of stairs to the court and return again, especially for one so indolent as herself; but there seemed to be no other way. She inwardly resolved to wreak additional vengeance upon Tom, and so get what satisfaction she could in this way. Muttering imprecations which I do not care to repeat, she started downstairs, determined to try the stick first upon Tim. But when she reached the court Tim had disappeared. He had divined her benevolent intentions, and thought it would be altogether wiser for him to be out of the way.

Granny picked up the stick, and, after a sharp glance around the court, commenced the ascent. She did not stop to rest, being spurred on by the anticipated pleasure of flogging Tom. So, in a briefer space of time than could have been expected, she once more arrived at her own door.

But Tom had not been idle.

No sooner was the door closed than Tom turned the key in the lock, making herself a voluntary prisoner, but having in the key the means of deliverance.

Granny tried the door, and, to her inexpressible wrath, discovered Tom's new audacity.

"Open the door, you trollop!" she screamed.

"You'll lick me," said Tom.

"I'll give you the wust lickin' you ever had."

"Then I shan't let you in," said Tom, defiantly.

CHAPTER IV
THE SIEGE.
"Open the door," screamed granny, beside herself with rage, "or I'll kill you."

"You can't get at me," said Tom, triumphantly.

The old woman grasped the knob of the door and shook it vigorously. But the lock resisted her efforts. Tom's spirit was up, and she rather enjoyed it.

"Shake away, granny," she called through the key-hole.

"If I could only get at you!" muttered granny.

"I won't let you in till you promise not to touch me."

"I'll skin you alive."

"Then you can't come in."

The old woman began alternately to pound and kick upon the door. Tom sat down coolly upon a chair, her dark eyes flashing exultingly. She knew her power, and meant to keep it. She had not reflected how it was to end. She supposed that in the end she would get a "lickin'," as she had often done before. But in the mean while she would have the pleasure of defying and keeping the old woman at bay for an indefinite time. So she sat in placid enjoyment in her stronghold until she heard something that suggested a speedy raising of the siege.

"I'm goin' for a hatchet," said granny, through the key-hole.

"If you break the door, you'll have to pay for it."

"Never you mind!" said the old woman. "I know what I'm about."

She heard the retreating steps of granny, and, knowing only too well her terrible temper, made up her mind that she was in earnest. If so, the door must soon succumb. A hatchet would soon accomplish what neither kicks nor pounding had been able to effect.

"What shall I do?" thought Tom.

She was afraid of something more than a lickin' now. In her rage at having been so long baffled, the old woman might attack her with the hatchet. She knew very well that on previous occasions she had flung at her head anything she could lay hold of. Tom, brave and stout-hearted as she was, shrunk from this new danger, and set herself to devise a way of escape. She looked out of the window; but she was on the fourth floor, and it was a long distance to the court below. If it had been on the second floor she would have swung off.

There was another thing she could do. Granny had gone down below to borrow a hatchet. She might unlock the door, and run out upon the landing; but there was no place for hiding herself, and no way of getting downstairs without running the risk of rushing into granny's clutches. In her perplexity her eyes fell upon a long coil of rope in one corner. It was a desperate expedient, but she resolved to swing out of the window, high as it was. She managed to fasten one end securely, and let the other drop from the window. As it hung, it fell short of reaching the ground by at least ten feet. But Tom was strong and active, and never hesitated a moment on this account. She was incited to extra speed, for she already heard the old woman ascending the stairs, probably provided with a hatchet.

Tom got on the window-sill, and, grasping the rope, let herself down rapidly hand over hand, till she reached the end of the rope. Then she dropped. It was rather hard to her feet, and she fell over. But she quickly recovered herself.

Tim, the recipient of her dinner, was in the court, and surveyed her descent with eyes and mouth wide open.

"Where'd you come from, Tom?" he asked.

"Can't you see?" said Tom.

"Why didn't you come downstairs?"

"'Cause granny's there waitin' to lick me. I must be goin' before she finds out where I am. Don't you tell of me, Tim."

"No, I won't," said Tim; and he was sure to keep his promise.

Tom sped through the arched passage to the street, and did not rest till she had got a mile away from the home which had so few attractions for her.

Beyond the chance of immediate danger, the young Arab conjured up the vision of granny's disappointment when she should break open the door, and find her gone; and she sat down on the curbstone and laughed heartily.

"What are you laughing at?" asked a boy, looking curiously at the strange figure before him.

"Oh, it's too rich!" said Tom, pausing a little, and then breaking out anew.

"What's too rich?"

"I've run away from granny. She wanted to lick me, and now she can't."

"You've been cutting up, I suppose."

"No, it's granny that's been cuttin' up. She's at it all the time."

"But you'll catch it when you do go home, you know."

"Maybe I won't go home."

It was not a street-boy that addressed her; but a boy with a comfortable home, who had a place in a store near by. He did not know, practically, what sort of a thing it was to wander about the streets, friendless and homeless; but it struck him vaguely that it must be decidedly uncomfortable. There was something in this strange creature—half boy in appearance—that excited his interest and curiosity, and he continued the conversation.

"What sort of a woman is your granny, as you call her?" he asked.

"She's an awful old woman," was the answer.

"I shouldn't think you would like to speak so of your grandmother."

"I don't believe she is my grandmother. I only call her so."

"What's your name?"

"Tom."

"Tom!" repeated the boy, in surprise. "Aint you a girl?"

"Yes; I expect so."

"It's hard to tell from your clothes, you know;" and he scanned Tom's queer figure attentively.

Tom was sitting on a low step with her knees nearly on a level with her chin, and her hands clasped around them. She had on her cap of the morning, and her jacket, which, by the way, had been given to granny when on a begging expedition, and appropriated to Tom's use, without special reference to her sex. Tom didn't care much. It made little difference to her whether she was in the fashion or not; and if the street boys chaffed her, she was abundantly able to give them back as good as they sent.

"What's the matter with my clothes?" said Tom.

"You've got on a boy's cap and jacket."

"I like it well enough. As long as it keeps a feller warm I don't mind."

"Do you call yourself a feller?"

"Yes."

"Then you're a queer feller."

"Don't you call me names, 'cause I won't stand it;" and Tom raised a pair of sharp, black eyes.

"I won't call you names, at least not any bad ones. Have you had any dinner?"

"Yes," said Tom, smacking her lips, as she recalled her delicious repast, "I had a square meal."

"What do you call a square meal?"

"Roast beef, cup o' coffee, and pie."

The boy was rather surprised, for such a dinner seemed beyond Tom's probable resources.

"Your granny don't treat you so badly, after all. That's just the kind of dinner I had."

"Granny didn't give it to me. I bought it. That's what she wants to lick me for. All she give me was a piece of hard bread."

"Where did you get the money? Was it hers?"

"That's what she says. But if a feller works all the mornin' for some money, hasn't she got a right to keep some of it?"

"I should think so."

"So should I," said Tom, decidedly.

"Have you got any money?"

"No, I spent it all for dinner."

"Then here's some."

The boy drew from his vest-pocket twenty-five cents, and offered it to Tom.

The young Arab felt no delicacy in accepting the pecuniary aid thus tendered.

"Thank you," said she. "You can call me names if you want to."

"What should I want to call you names for?" asked the boy, puzzled.

"There was a gent called me names this mornin', and give me twenty cents for doin' it."

"What did he call you?"

"I dunno; but it must have been something awful bad, it was so long."

"You're a strange girl, Tom."

"Am I? Well, I reckon I am. What's your name?"

"John Goodwin."

"John Goodwin?" repeated Tom, by way of fixing it in her memory.

"Yes; haven't you got any other name than Tom?"

"I dunno. I think granny called me Jane once. But it's a good while ago. Everybody calls me Tom, now."

"Well, Tom, I must be getting back to the store. Good-by. I hope you'll get along."

"All right!" said Tom. "I'm goin' into business with that money you give me."

CHAPTER V
TOM GAINS A VICTORY.

Granny mounted the stairs two at a time; so eager was she to force a surrender on the part of the rebellious Tom. She was a little out of breath when she reached the fourth landing, and paused an instant to recover it. Tom was at that moment half-way down the rope; but this she did not suspect.

Recovering her breath, she strode to the door. Before making an assault with the hatchet, she decided to summon Tom to a surrender.

"Tom!" she called out.

Of course there was no answer.

"Why don't you answer?" demanded granny, provoked.

She listened for a reply, but Tom remained obstinately silent, as she interpreted it.

"If you don't speak, it'll be the wuss for ye," growled granny.

Again no answer.

"I'll find a way to make you speak. Come and open the door, or I'll break it down. I've got a hatchet."

But the old woman had the conversation all to herself.

Quite beside herself now with anger, she no longer hesitated; but with all her force dealt a blow which buried the hatchet deep in the door.

"Jest wait till I get in!" she muttered. "Will ye open it now?"

But there was no response.

While she was still battering at the door one of the neighbors came up from below.

"What are you doin', Mrs. Walsh?" for such was granny's name.

"I'm tryin' to get in."

"Why don't you open the door?"

"Tom's locked it. She won't let me in," said granny, finishing the sentence with a string of profane words which had best be omitted.

"You'll have a good bill to pay to the landlord, Mrs. Walsh."

"I don't care," said granny. "I'm goin' to get at that trollop, and beat her within an inch of her life."

Another vigorous blow broke the lock, and the door flew open.

Granny rushed in, after the manner of a devouring lion ready to pounce upon her prey. But she stopped short in dismay. Tom was not visible!

Thinking she might be in the closet, the old woman flung open the door: but again she was balked.

"What has 'come of the child?" she exclaimed, in bewilderment.

"She got out of the window," said the neighbor, who had caught sight of the rope dangling from the open casement.

Granny hastened to the window, and the truth flashed upon her. Her prey had escaped her!

It was a deep disappointment to the vindictive old woman, whose hand itched to exercise itself in punishing Tom.

"She's a bold un," said the neighbor, with some admiration of Tom's pluck.

Granny answered with a strain of invective, which gave partial vent to the rage and disappointment she felt.

"If I could only get at her!" she muttered between her teeth; "I'd give her half-a-dozen lickin's in one. She'd wish she hadn't done it."

Not a doubt entered granny's mind that Tom would return. It never occurred to her that her young servant had become tired of her bondage, and had already made up her mind to break her chains. She knew Tom pretty well, but not wholly. She did not realize that the days of her rule were at an end; and that by her tyranny she had driven from her the girl whose earnings she had found so convenient.

If there had been much chance of meeting Tom outside, granny would have gone out into the streets and hunted for her. But to search for her among the numerous streets, lanes, and alleys in the lower part of the city would have been like trying to find a needle in a haystack. Then, even if she found her, she could not very well whip her in the street. Tom would probably come home at night as usual, bringing money, and she could defer the punishment till then.

Fatigued with her exercise and excitement, the old woman threw herself down on her rude pallet, first drawing the contents of a jug which stood in the closet, and was soon in a drunken sleep. Leaving her thus, we go back to Tom.

She had made up her mind not to go back to sweeping the streets; partly, indeed, because she no longer had her broom with her. Moreover, she thought that she would in that case be more likely to fall into the clutches of the enemy she so much dreaded. With the capital for which she was indebted to her new boy acquaintance she decided to lay in a supply of evening papers, and try to dispose of them. It was not a new trade to her; for there was scarcely one of the street trades in which the young Arab had not more or less experience.

She bought ten copies of the "Express," and selected the corner of two streets for the disposal of her stock in trade.

"Here's the 'Express,'—latest news from the seat of war!" cried Tom; catching the cry from a boy engaged in the same business up on Broadway.

"What's the news?" asked one of two young men who were passing.

"The news is that you're drafted," said Tom, promptly. "Buy the paper, and you'll find out all about it."

It was in the midst of the draft excitement in New York; and as it so happened that the young man had actually been drafted, his companion laughed.

"You must buy a paper for that, Jack," he said.

"I believe I will," said the first, laughing. "Here's ten cents. Never mind about the change."

"Thank you," said Tom. "Come round to-morrow, and I'll sell you another."

"You'll have me drafted again, I am afraid. Perhaps you will go as my substitute?"

"I would if I was old enough," said Tom.

"You're a girl,—aint you? Girls can't fight."

"Try me and see," said Tom. "I can fight any boy of my size."

The two young men passed on, laughing.

Tom soon had an opportunity to test her prowess. The corner where she had stationed herself was usually occupied by a boy somewhat larger than Tom, who considered that it belonged to him by right. He came up rather late, having a chance to carry a carpet-bag for a guest at French's Hotel to the Hudson River station. Tom had disposed of half her papers when he came blustering up:—

"Clear out of here!" he said, imperiously.

"Who was you speakin' to?" asked Tom, coolly.

"To you. Just clear out!"

"What for?" asked Tom.

"You've got my stand."

"Have I?" said Tom, not offering to move.

"Yes, you have."

"Then I'm goin' to keep it. 'Ere's the 'Express,'—latest news from the seat of war."

"Look here!" said the newsboy, menacingly, "if you don't clear out, I'll make you."

"Will you?" said Tom, independently, taking his measure, and deciding that she could fight him. "I aint afraid of you!"

Her rival advanced, and gave her a push which nearly thrust her from the sidewalk into the street. But he was rather astonished the next moment at receiving a blow in the face from Tom's fist.

"If you want to fight, come on!" said Tom, dropping her papers and squaring off.

He was not slow in accepting the defiance, being provoked by the unexpected blow, and aimed a blow at Tom's nose. But Tom, who had some rudimental ideas of boxing, while her opponent knew nothing of it, fended off the blow, and succeeded in getting in another.

"Ho! ho!" laughed another boy, who had just come up; "you're licked by a gal."

Bob, for this was the newsboy's name, felt all the disgrace of the situation. His face reddened, and he pitched in promiscuously, delivering blow after blow wildly. This gave a decided advantage to Tom, who inflicted considerably more damage than she received.

The fight would have gone on longer if a gentleman had not come up, and spoken authoritatively: "What is all this fighting about? Are you not ashamed to fight with a girl?"

"No, I aint," said Bob, sullenly. "She took my place, and wouldn't give it up."

"Is that true?" turning to Tom.

"I've got as much right to it as he," said Tom. "I'll give it to him if I am a gal."

"Don't you know it is wrong to fight?" asked the gentleman, this time addressing Tom.

"No, I don't," said Tom. "Wouldn't you fight if a feller pitched into you?"

This was rather an embarrassing question, but the gentleman said, "It would be better to go away than to get into a fight."

"He fit me."

"It is bad enough for boys to fight, but it is worse for girls."

"Don't see it," said Tom.

Had Tom been in a higher social position, it might have been suggested to her that to fight was not ladylike; but there was such an incongruity between Tom's appearance and anything lady-like, that such an appeal would have been out of place. The fact is, Tom claimed no immunity or privilege on the score of sex, but regarded herself, to all intents and purposes, as a boy, and strongly wished that she were one.

The gentleman looked at her, rather puzzled, and walked away, satisfied with having stopped the fight.

Bob did not seem inclined to renew hostilities, but crossed the street, and took his stand there. Tom, by right of conquest, held her place until she had sold out her whole stock of papers.

CHAPTER VI
AN UNFASHIONABLE HOTEL.

Tom found at the end of the afternoon that her capital had increased from twenty-five to fifty cents.

"Granny won't get none of this," she soliloquized, complacently. "It's all mine."

Sitting on a doorstep she counted over the money with an entirely different feeling from what she had experienced when it was to be transferred to granny. Now it was all her own, and, though but fifty cents, it made her feel rich.

"What shall I do with it?" thought Tom.

She had a square meal in the middle of the day; but several hours had passed since then, and she felt hungry again; Tom did not see any necessity for remaining hungry, with fifty cents in her possession. She made her way, therefore, to another eating-house, where the prices were the same with those at the one before mentioned, and partook of another square meal, leaving out the pie. This reduced her capital to thirty cents. She felt that she ought to save this, to start in business upon in the morning. As a street-sweeper she required no capital except her broom; but though Tom was not troubled with pride, she preferred to sell papers, or take up some other street vocation. Besides, she knew that as a street-sweeper on Broadway, she would be more likely to be discovered by the old woman whom she was now anxious to avoid.

After eating supper Tom went out into the streets, not knowing exactly how to spend her time. Usually, she had gone down into the court, or the street, and played with the children of her own and neighboring tenement houses. But now she did not care to venture back into the old locality.

So she strolled about the streets aimlessly, until she felt sleepy, and began to consider whereabouts to bestow herself for the night. She might have gone to the "Girls' Lodging House," if she had known of such an institution; but she had never heard of it. Chance brought her to a basement, on which was the sign,—

"LODGINGS—FIVE CENTS."

This attracted Tom's attention. If it had not been a cold night, she would have been willing to sleep out, which would have been cheaper; but it was a damp and chilly evening, and her dress was thin.

"Five cents won't bust me!" thought Tom. "I'll go in."

She went down some steps, and opened a door into a room very low-studded, and very dirty.

A stout woman, in a dirty calico loose-gown, was sitting in a chair, with a fat, unhealthy-looking baby in her lap.

"What you want, little gal?" she asked.

"Where's your lodgin'?" asked Tom.

"In back," answered the woman, pointing to an inner room, partially revealed through a half-open door. It was dark, having no windows, and dirtier, if possible, than the front room. The floor was covered with straw, for beds and bedsteads were looked upon as unnecessary luxuries in this economical lodging-house.

"Is that the place?" asked Tom.

"Yes. Do you want to stop here to-night?"

Tom had not been accustomed to first-class hotels, still the accommodations at granny's were rather better than this. However, the young Arab did not mind. She had no doubt she could sleep comfortably on the straw, and intimated her intention of stopping.

"Where's your money?" asked the woman.

The invariable rule in this establishment was payment in advance, and, perhaps, considering the character of the customers, it was the safest rule that could be adopted.

Tom took out her money, and counted out five cents into the woman's palm. She then put back the remainder in her pocket. If she had been less sleepy, she might have noticed the woman's covetous glance, and been led to doubt the safety of her small fortune. But Tom was sleepy, and her main idea was to go to bed as soon as possible.

"Lay down anywhere," said the landlady, dropping the five cents into her pocket.

Tom's preparation for bed did not take long. No undressing was required, for it was the custom here to sleep with the day's clothes on. Tom stowed herself away in a corner, and in five minutes was asleep.

It was but little after eight o'clock, and she was, at present, the only lodger.

No sooner did her deep, regular breathing indicate slumber, than the landlady began to indulge in various suspicious movements. She first put down her baby, and then taking a lantern,—the only light which could safely be carried into the lodging-room, on account of the straw upon the floor,—crept quietly into the inner room.

"She's fast asleep," she muttered.

She approached Tom with cautious step. She need not have been afraid to awaken her. Tom was a good sleeper, and not likely to wake up, unless roughly awakened, until morning.

Tom was lying on her side, with her face resting on one hand.

The woman stooped down, and began to look for the pocket in which she kept her money; but it was in that part of her dress upon which she was lying. This embarrassed the woman somewhat, but an idea occurred to her. She took up a straw, and, bending over, gently tickled Tom's ear. Tom shook her head, as a cat would under similar circumstances, and on its being repeated turned over, muttering, "Don't, granny!"

This was what her dishonest landlady wanted. She thrust her hand into Tom's pocket, and drew out the poor girl's entire worldly treasure. Tom, unconscious of the robbery, slept on; and the woman went back to the front room to wait for more lodgers. They began to come in about ten, and by twelve the room was full. It was a motley collection, and would have been a curious, though sad study, to any humane observer. They were most of them in the last stages of ill-fortune, yet among them was more than one who had once filled a respectable position in society. Here was a man of thirty-five, who ten years before had filled a good place, with a fair salary, in a city bank. But in an evil hour he helped himself to some of the funds of the bank. He lost his situation, and, though he escaped imprisonment, found his prospects blasted. So he had gone down hill, until at length he found himself reduced to such a lodging-house as this, fortunate if he could command the small sum needful to keep him from a night in the streets.

Next him was stretched a man who was deserving still more pity, since his misfortunes sprang rather from a want of judgment than from his own fault. He was a scholar, with a fair knowledge of Latin and Greek, and some ability as a writer. He was an Englishman who had come to the city in the hope of making his acquisitions available, but had met with very poor encouragement. He found that both among teachers and writers the demand exceeded the supply, at least for those of moderate qualifications; and, having no influential friends, had sought for employment almost in vain. His small stock of money dwindled, his suit became shabby, until he found himself, to his deep mortification and disgust, compelled to resort to such lodging-houses as this, where he was obliged to herd with the lowest and most abandoned class.

Next to him lay a mechanic, once in profitable employment. But drink had been his ruin; and now he was a vagabond, spending the little money he earned, at rum-shops, except what was absolutely necessary for food.

There is no need of cataloguing the remainder of Meg Morely's lodgers. Her low rates generally secured her a room-full, and a dozen, sometimes more, were usually packed away on the floor. On the whole she found it a paying business, though her charges were low. Sixty cents a day was quite a respectable addition to her income, and she had occupied the same place for two years already. Tom's experience will show that she had other, and not quite so lawful, ways of swelling her receipts, but she was cautious not to put them in practice, unless she considered it prudent, as in the present instance.

It was seven o'clock when Tom awoke. She looked around her in bewilderment, thinking at first she must be in granny's room. But a glance at the prostrate forms around her brought back the events of the day before, and gave her a realizing sense of her present situation.

"I've had a good sleep," said Tom to herself, stretching, by way of relief from her constrained position. "I guess it's time to get up."

She rubbed her eyes, and shook back her hair, and then rising, went into the front room. Her landlady was already up and getting breakfast.

"What time is it?" asked Tom.

"It's just gone seven," said Meg, looking sharply at Tom to see if she had discovered the loss of her money. "How did you sleep?"

"Tip-top."

"Come ag'in."

"All right!" said Tom. "Maybe I will."

She climbed up the basement stairs to the street above, and began to think of what the day had in store for her. Her prospects were not brilliant certainly; but Tom on the whole felt in good spirits. She had thrown off the yoke of slavery. She was her own mistress now, and granny's power was broken. Tom felt that she could get along somehow. She had confidence in herself, and was sure something would turn up for her.

"Now, what'll I do first?" thought Tom.

With twenty-five cents in her pocket, and a good appetite, breakfast naturally suggested itself.

She dove her hand into her pocket, but the face of the little Arab almost instantly expressed deep dismay.

Her money was gone!

CHAPTER VII.
TOM MAKES A FRIEND.

Twenty-five cents is not a large sum, but it was Tom's entire fortune. It was all she had, not only to buy breakfast with, but also to start in business. She had an excellent appetite, but now there was no hope of satisfying it until she could earn some more money.

Tom hurried back to the lodging, and entered, looking excited.

"Well, what's wanted?" asked Meg, who knew well enough without asking.

"I've lost some money."

"Suppose you did," said the woman, defiantly, "you don't mean to say I took it."

"No," said Tom, "but I had it when I laid down."

"Where was it?"

"In my pocket."

"Might have tumbled out among the straw," suggested Meg.

This struck Tom as not improbable, and she went back into the bedroom, and, getting down on her hands and knees, commenced poking about for it. But even if it had been there, any of my readers who has ever lost money in this way knows that it is very difficult to find under such circumstances.

Tom persevered in her search until her next-door neighbor growled out that he wished she would clear out. At length she was obliged to give it up.

"Have you found it?" asked Meg.

"No," said Tom, soberly.

"How much was it?"

"Twenty-five cents."

"That aint much."

"It's enough to bust me. I don't believe it's in the straw."

"What do you believe?" demanded Meg, whose guilty conscience made her scent an accusation.

"I think some of them took it while I was asleep," said Tom, indicating the other lodgers by a jerk of her finger.

"Likely they did," said Meg, glad to have suspicion diverted elsewhere.

"I wish I knew," said Tom.

"What'ud you do?"

"I'd get it back again," said Tom, her black eyes snapping with resolution.

"No, you wouldn't. You're nothin' but a babby. You couldn't do nothin'!"

"Couldn't I?" returned Tom. "I'd let 'em know whether I was a baby."

"Well, you go along now," said Meg. "Your money's gone, and you can't get it back. Next time give it to me to keep, and it'll be safe."

Being penniless, Tom was in considerable uncertainty when she would again be mistress of so large a sum. At present she felt in no particular dread of being robbed. She left the lodgings, realizing that the money was indeed gone beyond hope of recovery.

There is some comfort in beginning the day with a good breakfast. It warms one up, and inspires hope and confidence. As a general rule people are good-natured and cheerful after a hearty breakfast. For ten cents Tom might have got a cup of coffee, or what passed for such, and a plate of tea-biscuit. With the other fifteen she could have bought a few morning papers, and easily earned enough to pay for a square meal in the middle of the day. Now she must go to work without capital, and on an empty stomach, which was rather discouraging. She would have fared better than this at granny's, though not much, her breakfast there usually consisting of a piece of stale bread, with perhaps a fragment of cold sausage. Coffee, granny never indulged in, believing whiskey to be more healthful. Occasionally, in moments of extreme good nature, she had given Tom a sip of whiskey; but the young Arab had never got to like it, fortunately for herself, though she had accepted it as a variation of her usual beverage, cold water.

In considering what she should do for the day, Tom decided to go to some of the railway stations or steamboat landings, and try to get a chance to carry a carpet-bag. "Baggage-smashing" required no capital, and this was available in her present circumstances.

Tom made her way to the pier where the steamers of the Fall River line arrive. Ordinarily it would have been too late, but it had been a windy night, the sound was rough, and the steamer was late, so that Tom arrived just in the nick of time.

Tom took her place among the hackmen, and the men and boys who, like her, were bent on turning an honest penny by carrying baggage.

"Clear out of the way here, little gal!" said a stout, overgrown boy. "Smash your baggage, sir?"

"Clear out yourself!" said Tom, boldly. "I've got as much right here as you."

Her little, sharp eyes darted this way and that in search of a possible customer. The boy who had been rude to her got a job, and this gave Tom a better chance. She offered her services to a lady, who stared at her with curiosity and returned no answer. Tom began to think she should not get a job. There seemed a popular sentiment in favor of employing boys, and Tom, like others of her sex, found herself shut out from an employment for which she considered herself fitted. But, at length, she saw approaching a big, burly six-footer, with a good-natured face. There was something about him which inspired Tom with confidence, and, pressing forward, she said, "Carry your bag, sir?"

He stopped short and looked down at the queer figure of our heroine. Then, glancing at his carpet-bag, which was of unusual size and weight, the idea of his walking through the streets with Tom bending beneath the weight of his baggage, struck him in so ludicrous a manner that he burst into a hearty laugh.

"What's up?" demanded Tom, suspiciously. "Who are you laughin' at?"

"So you want to carry my carpet-bag?" he asked, laughing again.

"Yes," said Tom.

"Why, I could put you in it," said the tall man, his eyes twinkling with amusement.

"No, you couldn't," said Tom.

"Do you think you could carry it?"

"Let me try."

He set it down, and Tom lifted it from the ground; but it was obviously too much for her strength.

"You see you can't do it. Have you found anything to do this morning?"

"No," said Tom.

"Business isn't good, hey?"

"No," said Tom, "but I wouldn't mind so much if I hadn't had my money stole. I'm bust!"

"How's that? Did the bank break or have you been speculating?"

"Oh, you're gasin'! I aint got nothing to do with banks. Somebody stole two shillin's I had, so I've had no breakfast."

"Come, that's bad. I guess I must give you a job, after all. You can't carry my bag, but you can carry this."

He had under his arm something wrapped in a paper, making a small bundle. He handed it to Tom, and she trudged along with it after him.

"You couldn't guess what that is, I suppose?" said her companion, sociably.

"No," said Tom; "it feels soft."

"It's a large wax doll, for my little niece," said her patron. "You haven't got any dolls, I suppose?"

"I had one once," said Tom. "It was made of rags. But granny threw it into the fire."

"I suppose you were sorry."

"I was then; but I'm too old for dolls now."

"How old are you?"

"I aint sure. Somewheres about twelve."

"You live with your granny, then?"

"No, I don't,—not now."

"Why not?"

"She wanted to lick me, so I run away."

"Then where do you live now?"

"Nowhere."

"You have no home?"

"I don't want no home. I can take care of myself," said Tom, briskly.

"I see you are an independent, young woman. Now, if you were a boy, I'd give you a chance on board my ship."

"Have you got a ship?" asked Tom, becoming interested.

"Yes, I am a sea-captain, and go on long voyages. If you wasn't a girl, I'd take you along with me as cabin-boy."

"I wish you would," said Tom, eagerly.

"But you are a girl, you know? You couldn't climb a mast."

"Try me," said Tom. "I'm strong. I fit with a boy yesterday, and licked him." Captain Barnes laughed, but shook his head.

"I see you're spunky, if you are a girl," he said. "But I never heard of a girl being cabin-boy, and I don't think it would do."

"I'd put on a boy's clothes," suggested Tom.

"You've begun to do it already," said the captain, glancing at the cap and jacket. "I didn't know at first but you were a boy. What makes you wear a cap?"

"Granny gave it to me. I like it better than a bonnet."

They had by this time reached Broadway.

"You may steer across the Park to French's Hotel," said the sailor. "It's too late to get breakfast at my sister's."

"All right," said Tom.

They crossed the Park, and the street beyond, and reached the door of the brick hotel on the corner of Frankfort Street.

"I'll go down into the restaurant first," said Captain Barnes. "I feel like laying in a cargo before navigating any farther."

"Here's your bundle," said Tom.

He took it, and handed Tom twenty-five cents, which she received with gratification, not having expected so much for carrying so small a bundle.

"Stay a moment," said the sailor, as she was about to go away. "You haven't had any breakfast, I think you said."

"No."

"Then you shall come in, and breakfast with me."

This invitation astonished Tom not a little. It was the first invitation she had ever received to breakfast with a gentleman. French's restaurant being higher priced than those which her class were in the habit of patronizing, she entered with some hesitation, not feeling quite sure how her entrance would be regarded by the waiters. She was not generally wanting in self-possession, but as she descended the stairs and entered the room, she felt awkward and out of her element.

CHAPTER VIII.
AT FRENCH'S HOTEL.

"Clear out of here!" said a waiter, arresting Tom's progress, and pointing to the steps by which she had descended from the sidewalk.

If Tom had been alone, she would have felt bound to obey the summons; but being under the protection of Captain Barnes, who, she reflected, looked a good deal stronger than the waiter, she stood her ground.

"Did you hear what I said?" demanded the waiter angrily, about to take Tom by the shoulder.

"Avast there!" put in the captain, who thought it time to interfere; "is that the way you treat your customers?"

"She aint no customer."

"She is going to take breakfast here, my friend, and I should like to know what you have got to say about it."

The waiter seemed taken aback by this unexpected championship of one whom he had supposed to be an unprotected street girl.

"I didn't know she was with you," he stammered.

"Well, you know it now. Come, child, you can sit down here."

Tom enjoyed her triumph over the waiter, and showed it in a characteristic manner, by putting her thumb to her nose.

Captain Barnes sat down on one side of a table at one of the windows, and motioned Tom to sit opposite.

"I don't think you told me your name," he said.

"Tom."

"Then, Tom, let me suggest that you take off your cap. It's usual in the best society."

"I never was there," said Tom; but she removed her cap. This revealed a mop of hair, tangled it is true, but of a beautiful brown shade. Her black eyes sparkled from beneath, giving a bright, keen look to her face, browned by exposure to all weathers. I regret to say that the face was by no means clean. If it had been, and the whole expression had not been so wild and untamed, Tom would certainly have been considered pretty. As it was, probably no one would have wasted a second glance upon the little street girl.

"What will you have, sir, you and the young lady?" asked the waiter, emphasizing the last word, with a grin at Tom.

"What will you have, Tom?" asked the captain.

"Beefsteak, cup o' coffee, and bread-and-butter," said Tom, glibly.

Her knowledge of dishes was limited; but she had tried these and liked them, and this guided her in the selection.

"Very good," said Captain Barnes; "the same for me, with fried potatoes and an omelet."

Tom stared at this munificent order. She fixed her black eyes meditatively upon her entertainer, and wondered whether he always indulged in such a superlatively square meal.

"What are you thinking about, Tom?" questioned the captain.

"You must be awful rich," said Tom.

Captain Barnes laughed.

"What makes you think so?"

"It'll cost you a lot for breakfast."

"But you know I don't always have company to breakfast."

"Do you call me company?"

"Of course I do."

"I shouldn't think you'd want to have me eat with you."

"Why not?"

"You're a gentleman."

"And you're a young lady. Didn't you hear the waiter call you so?"

"He was chaffin'."

"You may be a lady some time."

"'Taint likely," said Tom.

"Why not?"

"I haven't got no good clothes to wear, nor don't know nothin'."

"Can you read?"

"A little, but I don't like to. It's too hard work."

"Makes your head ache, eh?"

"Yes," said Tom, seriously.

Captain Barnes looked attentively at the odd little creature opposite him. He wondered what would be her fate. She was quick, sharp, pretty, but withal an untamed Arab of the streets. The chances seemed very much against her in the warfare of life. Society seemed leagued against her, and she was likely to be at war with it.

"I'll make an effort to save her," he thought. But of this he did not speak to Tom at present, more especially as the waiter was seen advancing with the breakfast ordered.

He deposited the various dishes, some before Tom, and the remainder before the captain.

Tom was not used to restaurants of the better class, and did not see the necessity of an empty plate in addition to the dish which contained the meat. Such ceremony was not in vogue at the ten-cent restaurants which she had hitherto patronized. She fixed her eyes eagerly upon the beefsteak, which emitted a very savory odor.

"Pass your plate, Tom, and I will give you some meat."

Tom passed her plate, nothing loath, and the captain transferred to it a liberal supply of meat.

Tom waited for no ceremony, but, seizing her knife, attacked the meat vigorously.

"How is it?" asked her companion, amused.

"Bully!" said Tom, too busy to raise her eyes from her plate.

"Let me help you to a little of the omelet."

Tom extended her plate, and a portion of the omelet was placed upon it.

Tom raised a little to her lips, cautiously, for it was a new dish to her, and she did not know whether she would like it. It seemed to be satisfactory, however, none being left upon her plate when she had finished eating.

Not much conversation went on during the meal. Tom's entire energies were given to disposing of the squarest meal in which she had ever indulged, and the captain's attention was divided between his breakfast and the young waif upon whom he was bestowing perfect bliss.

At length Tom's efforts relaxed. She laid down her knife and fork, and heaved a sigh of exquisite enjoyment.

"Well," said the captain, "would you like some more?"

"No," said Tom, "I'm full."

"Did you enjoy your breakfast?"

"Didn't I, just?" and Tom's tone spoke volumes.

"I'm glad of that. I think it's very good myself."

"You're a brick!" said Tom, in a tone of grateful acknowledgment.

"Thank you," said Captain Barnes, his eyes twinkling a little; "I try to be."

"I wonder what granny would say if she knowed where I was," soliloquized Tom, aloud.

"She'd be glad you had enjoyed your breakfast."

"No, she wouldn't. She'd be mad."

"You don't give your grandmother a very good character. Doesn't she like you?"

"No; she hates me, and I hate her. She takes all my money, and then licks me."

"That's unpleasant, to be sure. Then you don't want to go back to her?"

"Not for Joe!" said Tom, shaking her head very decidedly.

"Then you expect to take care of yourself? Do you think you can?"

Tom nodded confidently.

"What are you going to do this morning, for instance?"

"Buy some papers with the money you give me."

"What a self-reliant spirit the little chit has!" thought Captain Barnes. "I've known plenty of young men, who had less faith in their ability to cope with the world, and gain a livelihood, than she. Yet she has next to no clothes, and her entire capital consists of twenty-five cents. There is a lesson for the timid and despondent in her philosophy."

Tom had no idea of what was passing in the mind of her companion. If she had been able to read his thoughts, it is not likely she would have understood them. Her own thoughts had become practical. She had had a good breakfast,—thanks to the kindness of her new friend,—but for dinner she must depend upon herself. She felt that it was quite time to enter upon the business of the day.

She put on her cap and rose to her feet.

"I'm goin'," she said, abruptly.

"Where are you going?"

"To buy some papers. Thank you for my breakfast."

It was probably the first time Tom ever thanked anybody for anything. I am not quite sure whether anybody before this had given her any cause for gratitude. Certainly, not granny, who had bestowed far less than she had received from the child, upon whom she had not been ashamed to be a selfish dependent. There was something, possibly, in her present companionship with a kind-hearted gentleman, something, perhaps, in her present more respectable surroundings, which had taught Tom this first lesson in good manners. She was almost surprised herself at the expression of gratitude to which she had given utterance.

"Stop a minute, Tom!" said the captain.

Tom had got half way to the door, but she stopped short on being called back.

"You haven't asked me whether I have got through with you."

Tom looked surprised. She knew of no further service in which she could make herself useful to her companion.

"Haven't you got through with me?" she asked.

"Not quite. I'm not going to stop here, you know,—I am going to my sister's."

"Where does she live?"

"In Sixteenth Street."

"Do you want me to carry your carpet-bag?" asked Tom.

"Well, no; I think you couldn't manage that. But you can carry the bundle."

"All right!" said Tom.

It was all one to her whether she sold papers, or carried bundles. The main thing was to earn the small amount of money necessary to defray her daily expenses. Of the two she would rather go up to Sixteenth Street; for as she had seldom found occasion to go up town, the expedition promised a little novelty.

Captain Barnes paid his bill, and left the restaurant, with Tom at his heels.

CHAPTER IX.
MRS. MERTON.

"We'll go across Broadway, and take the Sixth Avenue cars, Tom," said the captain.

"Are we goin' to ride?" asked Tom, surprised.

"Yes, you don't catch me lugging this heavy carpet-bag up to Sixteenth Street."

Tom was rather surprised at this. She did not understand why her services were required to carry the bundle if they were going to ride. However, she very sensibly remained silent, not feeling called upon to comment on her employer's arrangements.

At this time in the day there was no difficulty in obtaining a seat in the cars. Tom, however, was not disposed to sit down quietly:—

"I'll stand outside," she said.

"Very well," said Captain Barnes, and he drew out a copy of a morning paper which he had purchased on leaving the hotel.

Tom took her position beside the driver. She rather enjoyed the ride, for, though she had lived in the city for years, she had seldom been on the car as a passenger, though she had frequently stolen a ride on the steps of a Broadway omnibus.

"Well, Johnny, are you going up town to look after your family?" asked the driver, good-naturedly.

"I'd have to look a long time before I found 'em," said Tom.

"Haven't you got any relations, then?"

"There's an old woman that calls herself my granny."

"Does she live up on Fifth Avenue?"

"Yes," said Tom; "next door to you."

"You've got me there," said the driver, laughing. "Give my respects to your granny, and tell her she's got a smart grand-daughter."

"I will, when I see her."

"Don't you live with her?"

"Not now. She aint my style."

Here the conductor tapped Tom on the shoulder.

"He pays for me," said Tom, pointing back at Captain Barnes.

"I suppose he's your grandfather," said the driver, jocosely.

"I wish he was. He's a trump. He gave me a stunnin' breakfast."

"So you like him better than your granny?"

"You can bet on that."

Captain Barnes, sitting near the door, heard a part of this conversation, and it amused him.

"I wonder," he thought, "whether my sister will be willing to assume charge of this wild little girl? There's enough in her to make a very smart woman, if she is placed under the right influences and properly trained. But I suspect that will require not a little patience and tact. Well, we shall see."

After a while the car reached Sixteenth Street, and the captain left it, with Tom following him. They turned down Sixteenth Street from the avenue, and finally stopped before a fair-looking brick house. Captain Barnes went up the steps, and rang the bell.

"Is Mrs. Merton at home?" he asked.

"Yes," said the servant, looking hard at Tom.

"Then I'll come in. Tell her her brother wishes to see her. Come in, Tom."

Tom followed the captain, the servant continuing to eye her suspiciously. They entered the parlor, where Captain Barnes took a seat on the sofa, motioning Tom to sit beside him. Tom obeyed, surveying the sofa with some curiosity. The families in the tenement house with whom she had been on visiting terms did not in general possess sofas. She had sometimes seen them in furniture stores, but this was the first time she had sat upon one.

"What are you thinking of, Tom?" asked the captain, desiring to draw her out.

"Does your sister live here?"

"Yes."

"She's rich, isn't she?"

"No, she makes a living by keeping boarders. Perhaps you'd like to board with her."

Tom laughed.

"She don't take the likes of me," she said.

"Suppose you were rich enough, wouldn't you like to board here?"

"I don't know," said Tom, looking round. "It's dark."

"All the rooms are not dark. Besides, you'd get three square meals every day."

"I'd like that," said Tom, seriously.

Their further conversation was interrupted by the entrance of the captain's sister, Mrs. Merton. She was rather a stout woman, but there was an expression of care on her face, which was not surprising, for it is no light thing to keep a New York boarding-house.

"When did you arrive in the city, Albert?" she asked, giving him her hand cordially.

"Only just arrived, Martha. How does the world use you?"

"I can't complain, though it's a wearing thing looking after a household like this. Have you had any breakfast?"

"I took some down town."

Just then Mrs. Merton's eye fell for the first time upon Tom. She started in surprise, and looked doubtfully at her brother.

"Who is this?" she asked. "Did she come with you?"

"It's a young friend of mine. She met me at the wharf, and wanted to carry my carpet-bag."

"You didn't let her do it?"

"Bless you, no. It's big enough to pack her away in. But I employed her to carry a bundle. Didn't I, Tom?"

"What did you call her?" asked his sister.

"Tom. That's her name, so she says."

"What made you bring her here?" asked Mrs. Merton, who evidently regarded her brother's conduct as very queer.

"I'll tell you, but not before her. Tom, you can go out into the entry, and shut the door behind you. I'll call you in a few minutes."

Tom went out, and Captain Barnes returned to the subject.

"She's got no relations except an intemperate old grandmother," he said. "I've taken a fancy to her, and want to help her along. Can't you find a place for her in your kitchen?"

"I take a girl from the street!" ejaculated Mrs. Merton. "Albert, you must be crazy."

"Not at all. I am sure you can find something for her to do,—cleaning knives, running of errands, going to market, or something of that kind."

"This is a very strange proposal."

"Why is it? At present she lives in the street, being driven from the only home she had, by the ill-treatment of a vicious grandmother. You can see what chance she has of growing up respectably."

"But there are plenty such. I don't see that it's our business to look after them."

"I don't know why it is, but I've taken a fancy to this little girl."

"She looks perfectly wild."

"I won't deny that she is rather uncivilized, but there's a good deal in her. She's as smart as a steel trap."

"Smart enough to steal, probably."

"Perhaps so, under temptation. I want to remove the temptation."

"This is a very strange freak on your part, Albert."

"I don't know about that. You know I have no child of my own, and am well off, so far as this world's goods are concerned. I have long thought I should like to train up a child in whom I could take an interest, and who would be a comfort to me when I am older."

"You can find plenty of attractive children without going into the street for them."

"I don't want a tame child. She wouldn't interest me. This girl has spirit. I'll tell you what I want you to do, Martha. I'm going off on a year's voyage. Take her into your house, make her as useful as you can, civilize her, and I will allow you a fair price for her board."

"Do you want her to go to school?"

"After a while. At present she needs to be civilized. She is a young street Arab with very elementary ideas as to the way in which people live. She needs an apprenticeship in some house like this. My little niece must be about her age."

"Mary? How can I trust her to the companionship of such a girl?"

"Tom isn't bad. She is only untrained. She will learn more than she will teach at first. Afterwards Mary may learn something of her."

"I am sure I don't know what to say," said Mrs. Merton, irresolutely.

Here the captain named the terms he was willing to pay for Tom's board. This was a consideration to Mrs. Merton, who found that she had to calculate pretty closely to make keeping boarders pay.

"I'll try her," she said.

"Thank you, Martha. You can let her go into the kitchen at first, till she is fit to be promoted."

"She must have some clothes. She had on a boy's jacket."

"Yes, and cap. In fact she is more of a boy than a girl at present."

"I am not sure but some of Mary's old dresses may fit her. Mary must be a little larger than she is."

"That reminds me I brought a doll for Fanny. She has not grown too large for dolls yet."

"No, she is just the age to enjoy them. She will be delighted."

"I think we may call in Tom now, and inform her of our intention."

"She must have another name. It won't do to call a girl Tom."

"She said her name used to be Jenny, but she has been nicknamed Tom."

The door was opened, and Captain Barnes called in Tom.

"Come in, Tom," he said.

"All right!" said Tom. "I'm on hand!"

"We've been talking about you, Tom," pursued the captain.

"What have you been sayin'?" asked Tom, suspiciously.

"I've been telling my sister that you had no home, and were obliged to earn your own living in the streets."

"I don't care much," said Tom. "I'd rather do that than live with granny, and get licked."

"But wouldn't you like better to have a nice home, where you would have plenty to eat, and a good bed to sleep in?"

"Maybe I would."

"I've been asking my sister to let you stay here with her. Would you like that?"

Tom regarded Mrs. Merton attentively. The face was careworn, but very different from granny's. On the whole, it inspired her with some degree of confidence.

"If she wouldn't lick me very often," she said.

"How about that, Martha?" he asked.

"I think I can promise that," said Mrs. Merton, amused in spite of herself.

"Of course you will have to work. My sister will find something for you to do."

"I aint afraid of work," said Tom, "if I only get enough to eat, and aint licked."

"You see, Tom, I feel an interest in you."

"You're a brick!" said Tom, gratefully.

"Little girl," said Mrs. Merton, shocked, "you mustn't use such language in addressing my brother."

"Never mind, Martha; she means it as a compliment."

"A compliment to call you a brick!"

"Certainly. But now about clothes. Can't you rig her out with something that will make her presentable?"

"She needs a good washing first," said Mrs. Merton, surveying Tom's dirty face and hands with disfavor.

"A very good suggestion. You won't mind being washed, I suppose, Tom?"

"I'd just as lives," said Tom.

In fact she was quite indifferent on the subject. She was used to being dirty, but if she could oblige her new protector by washing, she was quite willing.

"I've got to go out for an hour or two," said Captain Barnes, "but I will leave my carpet-bag here, and come back to lunch."

"Of course, Albert. When do you sail?"

"In three days at farthest."

"Of course you will remain here up to the day of sailing."

"Yes, if you can find a spare corner to stow me in."

"It would be odd if I couldn't find room for my only brother."

"So be it, then. You may expect me."

He rose and taking his hat left the house. Tom and Mrs. Merton were now alone.

CHAPTER X.
TOM DROPS HER TATTERS.
"Now, what is your name, little girl?" asked Mrs. Merton, surveying Tom doubtfully, half sorry that she had undertaken the care of her.

"Tom."

"That's a boy's name."

"Everybody calls me Tom,—sometimes Tattered Tom."

"There's some reason about the first name," thought Mrs. Merton, as her glance rested on the ragged skirt and well-ventilated jacket of her brother's protegée.

"As you are a girl, it is not proper that you should have a boy's name. What is your real name?"

"I think it's Jenny. Granny used to call me so long ago, but I like Tom best."

"Then I shall call you Jenny. Now, Jenny, the first thing to do, is to wash yourself clean. Follow me."

Mrs. Merton went up the front stairs, and Tom followed, using her eyes to good advantage as she advanced.

The landlady led the way into a bath-room. She set the water to running, and bade Tom undress.

"Am I to get into the tub?" asked Tom.

"Yes, certainly. While you are undressing, I will try and find some clothes that will fit you."

Though she did not at first fancy the idea of bathing, Tom grew to like it, and submitted with a good grace. Mrs. Merton took care that it should be thorough. After it, she dressed Tom in some clothes, still very good, which had been laid aside by her daughter Mary. Then she combed Tom's tangled locks, and was astonished by the improvement it made in the appearance of the little waif.

I have already said that Tom had elements of beauty, but it took sharp eyes to detect them under the rags and dirt which had so effectually disguised her. She had very brilliant dark eyes, and a clear olive complexion, with cheeks that had a tinge of red instead of the pallor usually to be found in those children who have the misfortune to be reared in a tenement house. In her new clothes she looked positively handsome, as Mrs. Merton thought, though she did not see fit to say so to Tom herself.

When her toilet was concluded she turned Tom to the glass, and said, "There, Jenny, do you know who that is?"

Tom stared in open-eyed wonder at the image which she saw. She could hardly believe the testimony of her eyes.

"Is that me?" she asked.

"I believe so," said Mrs. Merton, smiling.

"It don't look like me a bit," continued Tom.

"It doesn't look like 'Tattered Tom,' certainly. Don't you like it better?"

"I dunno," said Tom, doubtfully. "It looks too much like a girl."

"But you are a girl, you know."

"I wish I wasn't."

"Why?"

"Boys have more fun; besides, they are stronger, and can fight better."

"But you don't want to fight?" said Mrs. Merton, scandalized.

"I licked a boy yesterday," said Tom, proudly.

"Why did you do that?"

"He sassed me, and I licked him. He was bigger'n I was, too!"

"I can't allow you to fight in future, Jenny," said Mrs. Merton. "It isn't at all proper for girls, or indeed for boys, to fight; but it is worse for girls."

"Why is it?" asked Tom.

"Because girls should be gentle and lady-like."

"If you was a girl, and a boy should slap you in the face, what would you do?" asked Tom, fixing her bright eyes upon her mentor.

"I should forgive him, and hope he would become a better boy."

"I wouldn't," said Tom. "I'd give him Hail Columby."

"You've got some very wrong ideas, Jenny," said Mrs. Merton. "I fear that your grandmother has not brought you up properly."

"She did not bring me up at all. I brought myself up. As for granny, she didn't care as long as I brought her money to buy whiskey."

Mrs. Merton shook her head. It was very evident to her that Tom had been under very bad influences.

"I hope you will see the error of your ways after a while, Jenny. My brother takes an interest in you, and for his sake I hope you will try to improve."

"If he wants me to, I will," said Tom, decidedly.

Arab as she was, she had been impressed by the kindness of Captain Barnes, and felt that she should like to please him. Still, there was a fascination in the wild independence of her street life which was likely for some time to interfere with her enjoyment of the usages of a more civilized state. There was little prospect of her taming down into an average girl all at once. The change must come slowly.

"My brother will be very much pleased if he finds that you have improved when he returns from his voyage."

"When is he goin' to sea?"

"In two or three days."

"I asked him to take me with him," said Tom; "but he wouldn't."

"You would only be in the way on a ship, Jenny."

"No, I shouldn't. I could be a cabin-boy."

"But you are not a boy."

"I could climb the masts as well as a boy. If there was only a pole here, I'd show you."

"What a child you are!"

"Did you ever read about the female pirate captain?" asked Tom.

"No."

"Jim Morgan told me all about it. He'd read it in some book. It was a bully story."

"Such stories are not fit to read."

"I'd like to be a pirate captain," said Tom, thoughtfully.

"You mustn't talk so, Jenny," said Mrs. Merton, shocked.

"But I would, though, and carry two pistols and a dagger in my belt, and then if anybody sassed me I'd give 'em all they wanted."

"My brother wouldn't like to hear you talk so, Jenny. I'm sure I don't know what has got into you to say such dreadful things."

"Then I won't," said Tom. "I wonder what granny would say if she saw me in these fixin's. She wouldn't know me."

"When my brother comes, you shall go down and open the door for him, and see if he knows you."

"That will be bully."

"Now I must be thinking what I can find for you to do. You will be willing to help me?"

"Yes," said Tom, promptly.

"Do you know how to make beds?"

"I can learn," said Tom.

"Didn't your grandmother ever teach you?" asked Mrs. Merton, who, though for a long time a resident of New York, had a very imperfect knowledge of how the poorest classes lived.

"Granny never made her bed," said Tom. "She just gave it a shake, and tumbled into it."

"Bless me, how shiftless she must be!" ejaculated Mrs. Merton, in surprise.

"Oh, granny don't mind!" said Tom, carelessly.

"Did you ever sweep?"

"Lots of times. That's the way I got money to carry to granny."

"Were you paid for sweeping, then?" asked Mrs. Merton.

"Yes, people that came along would give me money. If they wouldn't I'd muddy their boots."

"What do you mean, child? Where did you sweep?"

"Corner of Broadway and Chambers' Streets."

"Oh, you swept the crossing, then."

"In course I did. If you'll give me a broom, I'll go out and sweep front of your house; but I guess there aint so many people come along here as in Broadway."

"I don't want you to do that," said Mrs. Merton, hastily. "I want you to sweep the rooms in the house. Sarah, the chambermaid, will show you how, and also teach you to make beds."

"All right," said Tom. "Bring her on, and I'll help her."

"We will defer that till to-morrow. Now you may come down to the kitchen with me, and I'll see if I can find anything for you to do there."

Tom felt ready for any enterprise, and started to follow Mrs. Merton downstairs, but rather startled the good lady by making a rapid descent astride the banisters.

"Don't you do that again, Jenny," she said reprovingly.

"Why not?" asked Tom. "It's jolly fun."

CHAPTER XI
THE MISTAKES OF A MORNING.
On the way to the kitchen they met Sarah, the chambermaid, going upstairs to make the beds.

"Sarah," said Mrs. Merton, "here is a little girl who is going to stay with me, and help about the house. You may take her upstairs, and show her how to help you make the beds."

If Tom had been in her street costume, Sarah would have preferred to dispense with her assistance, but she looked quite civilized and respectable now, and she accepted the offer. Tom accompanied her upstairs to the second floor. The first chamber was that of Mr. Craven,—a gentleman in business down town. It was of course vacant, therefore.

Tom looked about her curiously.

"Now," said Sarah, "do you know anything about making beds?"

"No," said Tom.

"Then stand on one side, and I will tell you what to do."

Tom followed directions pretty well, but, as the task was about finished, an impish freak seized her, and she caught the pillow and threw it at Sarah's head, disarranging that young lady's hair, and knocking out a comb.

"What's that for?" demanded Sarah, angrily.

Tom sat down and laughed boisterously.

"It's bully fun!" she said. "Throw it at me."

"I'll give you a shaking, you young imp," said Sarah. "You've broke my comb."

She picked up the comb, and dashed round the bed after Tom, who, seeing no other way for escape, sprang upon the bed, where she remained standing.

"Come down from there," demanded Sarah.

"Let me alone, then!"

"I'll tell the missis, just as sure as you live!"

"What'll she do? Will she lick me?"

"You'll see."

This would not have checked Tom, but it occurred to her, all at once, that her freak would be reported to the captain, and might displease him.

"I'll stop," said she. "I was only in fun."

By this time, Sarah had ascertained that the comb was not broken, after all, and this made her more inclined to overlook Tom's offence.

"Now behave decent!" she said.

She gave Tom further directions about the proper way of doing chamber-work, which Tom followed quite closely, being resolved apparently to turn over a new leaf. But her reformation was not thorough. She caught sight of Mr. Craven's shaving materials, which he had carelessly left on the bureau, and before Sarah anticipated her intention, she had seized the brush and spread the lather over her cheeks.

"What are you doing, you little torment?" asked Sarah.

"I'm goin' to shave," said Tom. "It must feel funny."

"Put that razor down!" said Sarah, approaching.

Tom brandished the razor playfully, in a manner that considerably startled the chamber-maid, who stopped short in alarm:—

"I'll go and tell the missis how you cut up," said she, going to the door.

This was unnecessary, however, for at this moment Mrs. Merton, desirous of learning how Tom was getting along, opened the door. She started back in dismay at the spectacle which greeted her view, and, in a tone unusually decided for so mild a woman, said, "Jenny, put down that razor instantly, and wipe the soap from your cheeks. Not so," she added hastily, seeing that Tom was about to wipe it off upon her skirt. "Here, take the towel. Now, what do you mean by such conduct?"

"Wouldn't he like it?" asked Tom, somewhat abashed.

"Do you mean my brother?"

"Yes, the sailor man."

"No, he would be very angry."

"Then I won't do so again;" and Tom seemed quite decided in her repentance.

"What possessed you to touch those things, Jenny?"

"That isn't all she did, mum," said Sarah. "She threw the pillow at me, and almost druv the comb into my head. She's the craziest creetur' I ever sot eyes on."

"Did you do that?" asked Mrs. Merton.

"Yes," said Tom. "I told her she might pitch it at me. It's bully fun."

"I can't allow such goings-on," said Mrs. Merton. "If you do so again, I must send you back to your grandmother."

"You don't know where she lives," said Tom.

"At any rate I won't keep you here."

Tom thought of the three square meals which she would receive daily, and decided to remain. She continued quiet, therefore, and really helped Sarah in the remaining rooms. When this task was completed she went downstairs. At this moment a ring was heard at the door-bell. Thinking that it might be the captain, Tom answered the summons herself. She opened the door suddenly, but found herself mistaken.

A young gentleman was the visitor.

"Can I see Mrs. Merton?" he inquired.

"Yes," said Tom; "come in."

He stepped into the hall.

"Come right along. I'll show you where she is."

She knew that the landlady was in the kitchen, and supposed that this was the proper place to lead the visitor.

The latter followed Tom as far as the head of the stairs, and then paused.

"Where are you leading me?" he asked.

"She's down in the kitchen. Come right along."

"No, I will stay here. You may tell her there is a gentleman wishes to see her."

Tom went down, and found the landlady.

"There's a feller upstairs wants to see you," she said. "He wouldn't come down here. I asked him."

"Good gracious! You didn't invite him down into the kitchen?"

"Why not?" said Tom.

"You should have carried him into the parlor."

"All right!" said Tom. "I'll know better next time."

Mrs. Merton smoothed her hair, and went upstairs to greet her visitor, who proved to be an applicant for board.

Only fifteen minutes later Tom had a chance to improve on her first mistake. Again the door-bell rang, and again Tom opened the door. A wrinkled old woman, with a large basket, stood before her.

"I'm a poor widder," she whined, "with four childer that have nothing to ate. Can't you give me a few pennies, and may the blessings of Heaven rest upon you!"

"Come in," said Tom.

The old woman stepped into the hall.

"Come right in here," said Tom, opening the door of the parlor.

The old beggar, not accustomed to being received with so much attention, paused doubtfully.

"Come in, if you're comin'," said Tom, impatiently. "The lady told me to put everybody in here."

The old woman followed, and took a seat on the edge of a sofa, placing her basket on the carpet. Before Tom had a chance to acquaint her mistress with the fact that a visitor awaited her, the bell rang again. This time Tom found herself confronted by a fashionably dressed and imposing-looking lady.

"I wish to see Mrs. Merton," she said.

"All right!" said Tom. "Just you come in, and I'll call her."

The visitor entered, and was ushered also into the parlor. Leaving her to find a seat for herself, Tom disappeared in pursuit of the landlady.

Mrs. Courtenay did not at first observe the other occupant of the room. When her eyes rested on the old crone sitting on the sofa, with her basket, which was partly stored with cold victuals, resting on the carpet, she started in mingled astonishment and disgust. Her aristocratic nostrils curved, and, taking a delicate handkerchief, she tried to shut out the unsavory presence. The old woman saw the action, and fidgeted nervously, feeling that she ought not to be there. While the two guests were in this uncomfortable state of feeling, Mrs. Merton, quite unsuspicious of anything wrong, opened the door.

"Is this Mrs. Merton?" asked Mrs. Courtenay.

"Yes, madam."

"I called to inquire about a servant who referred me to you," continued Mrs. Courtenay, haughtily; "but I didn't anticipate the company I should find myself in."

Following her glance, Mrs. Merton was struck with dismay, as she saw the second visitor.

"How came you here?" she demanded hastily.

"The little gal brought me. It wasn't my fault indeed, mum," whined the old woman.

"What do you want?"

"I'm a poor widder, mum. If you could be so kind as to give me a few pennies."

"I have nothing for you to-day. You can go," said Mrs. Merton, who was too provoked to be charitable, as otherwise she might have been. She pointed to the door, and the applicant for charity hobbled out hastily, feeling that she was not likely to obtain anything under present circumstances.

"I must beg your pardon," said Mrs. Merton, "for the mistake of an inexperienced child, who has never before waited upon the door; though, how she could have made such an absurd blunder, I cannot tell."

Mrs. Courtenay deigned to be appeased, and opened her business. When she had left the house, Mrs. Merton called Tom.

"Jenny," she said, "how came you to show that beggar into the parlor?"

"She asked for you," said Tom, "and you told me to take everybody that asked for you into the parlor."

"Never take such a woman as that in."

"All right!" said Tom.

"That comes of taking a girl in from the street," thought Mrs. Merton. "I wish I hadn't agreed to take her."

CHAPTER XII
THE VANQUISHED BULLY.

Notwithstanding Tom's mistake, she was still intrusted with the duty of answering the bell. At length, to her satisfaction, she opened the door to her friend of the morning.

He looked at her in surprise.

"What, is this Tom?" he asked.

"Yes," she said, enjoying his surprise. "Didn't you know me?"

"Hardly. Why, you look like a young lady!"

"Do I?" said Tom, hardly knowing whether or not to feel pleased at the compliment, for she fancied she should prefer to be a boy.

"Yes, you are much improved. And how have you been getting on this morning?"

"I've been cutting up," said Tom, shaking her head.

"Not badly, I hope."

"I'll tell you what I did;" and Tom in her own way gave an account of the events related in the previous chapter.

The captain laughed heartily.

"You aint mad?" questioned Tom.

"Did you think I would be?"

"She said so," said Tom.

"Who is she?"

"Your sister."

The captain recovered his gravity. He saw that his merriment might encourage Tom in her pranks, and so increase the difficulties his sister was likely to find with her.

"No, I am not angry," he said, "but I want you very much to improve. You will have a good home here, and I want you to do as well as you can, so that when I get home from my voyage I may find you very much improved. Do you think I shall?"

Tom listened attentively.

"What do you want me to do?" she asked.

"To learn, as fast as you can, both about work and study. I shall leave directions to have you sent to school. Will you like that?"

"I don't know," said Tom. "I'm afraid I'll be bad, and get licked."

"Then try not to be bad. But you want to know something when you grow up,—don't you?"

"Yes."

"Then you will have to go to school and study. Can you read?"

"Not enough to hurt me," said Tom.

"Then, if you find yourself behind the rest, you must work all the harder. Will you promise me to do it?"

Tom nodded.

"And will you try to behave well?"

"Yes," said Tom. "I'll do it for you. I wouldn't do it for granny."

"Then do it for me."

Here Mrs. Merton appeared on the scene, and Tom was directed to go downstairs to assist the cook.

"Well, what do you think of her, Martha?"

"She's a regular trial. I'll tell you what she did this morning."

"I know all."

"Did she tell you?" asked his sister, in surprise.

"Yes, she voluntarily told me that she had been 'cutting up;' and, on my questioning her, confessed how. However, it was partly the result of ignorance."

"I wish I hadn't undertaken the charge of her."

"Don't be discouraged, Martha. There's some good in her, and she's as smart as a steel trap. She's promised me to turn over a new leaf, and do as well as she can."

"Do you rely upon that?"

"I do. She's got will and resolution, and I believe she means what she says."

"I hope it'll prove so," said Mrs. Merton, doubtfully.

"I find she knows very little. I should like to have her sent to school as soon as possible. She can assist you when at home, and I will take care that you lose nothing by it."

To this Mrs. Merton was brought to agree, but could not help expressing her surprise at the interest which her brother took in that child. She was a good woman, but it was not strange if the thought should come to her that she had two daughters of her own, having a better claim upon their uncle's money than this wild girl whom he had picked up in the streets. But Captain Barnes showed that he had not forgotten his nieces, as two handsome dress-patterns, sent in from Stewart's during the afternoon, sufficiently evinced.

Tom had not yet met Mrs. Merton's daughters, both being absent at school. They returned home about three o'clock. Mary, a girl of about Tom's age, had rather pretty, but insipid, features, and was vain of what she regarded as her beauty. Fanny, who was eight, was more attractive.

"Children, can't you speak to your uncle?" said Mrs. Merton; for the captain declared himself tired, and did not go out after lunch.

"How do you do, uncle?" said Mary, advancing and offering her hand.

"Why, Mary, you have become quite a young lady," said her uncle.

Mary simpered and looked pleased.

"And Fanny too. Martha, where is that doll I brought for her?"

The doll was handed to the delighted child.

"I suppose you are too old for dolls, Mary," said the captain to his eldest niece.

"I should think so, Uncle Albert," answered Mary, bridling.

"Then it's lucky I didn't bring you one. But I've brought you a playmate."

Mary looked surprised.

Tom was passing through the hall at the moment, and her guardian called her.

"Come in, Tom."

Mary Merton stared at the new-comer, and her quick eyes detected that the dress in which she appeared was one of her own.

"Why, she's got on my dress," she said.

"She is about your size, Mary, so I gave her your dress."

"Didn't she have any clothes of her own?"

"Were you unwilling to let her have that dress?" asked her uncle.

Mary pouted, and Captain Barnes said, "Martha, I will put money in your hands to supply Jenny with a suitable wardrobe. I had intended to give Mary new articles for all which been appropriated to Tom's use; but I have changed my mind."

"She can have them," said Mary, regretting her selfishness, from an equally selfish motive.

"I won't trouble you," said her uncle, rather coldly.

Tom had listened attentively to this conversation, turning her bright eyes from one to the other.

"Come here, Tom, and shake hands with these two little girls."

"I'll shake hands with her," said Tom, indicating Fanny.

"And won't you shake hands with Mary?"

"I don't want to."

"Why not?"

"I don't like her."

"Shake hands with her, for my sake."

Tom instantly extended her hand, but now it was Mary who held back. Her mother would have forced her to give her hand, but Captain Barnes said, "It don't matter. Leave them to become friends in their own time."

Two days afterwards the captain sailed. Tom renewed her promise to be a good girl, and he went away hopeful that she would keep it.

"I shall have somebody to come home to, Jenny," he said. "Will you be glad to see me back?"

"Yes, I will," she said; and there was a heartiness in her tone which showed that she meant what she said.

The next day Tom went to school. She was provided with two or three books such as she would need, and accompanied Fanny; for, though several years older, she was not as proficient as the latter.

In the next street there was a boy, whose pleasure it was to bully children smaller than himself. He had more than once annoyed Fanny, and when the latter saw him a little in advance, she said, nervously, "Let us cross the street, Jenny."

"Why?" asked Tom.

"There's George Griffiths just ahead."

"What if he is?"

"He's an awful bad boy. Sometimes he pulls away my books, and runs away with them. He likes to plague us."

"He'd better not try it," said Tom.

"What would you do?" asked Fanny, in surprise.

"You'll see. I won't cross the street. I'm goin' right ahead."

Fanny caught her companion's arm, and advanced, trembling, hoping that George Griffiths might not see them. But he had already espied them, and, feeling in a bullying mood, winked to a companion and said, "You'll see how I'll frighten these girls."

He advanced to meet them, and took off his hat with mock politeness.

"How do you do this morning, young ladies?" he said.

"Go away, you bad boy!" said little Fanny, in a flutter.

"I'll pay you for that," he said, and tried to snatch one of her books, but was considerably startled at receiving a blow on the side of the head from her companion.

"Just let her alone," said Tom.

"What have you got to say about it?" he demanded insolently.

"You'll see."

Hereupon he turned his attention to Tom, and tried to snatch her books, but was rather astounded when his intended victim struck him a sounding blow in the face with her fist.

"Take my books, Fanny," she said, and, dropping them on the sidewalk, squared off scientifically.

"Come on, if you want to!" said Tom, her eyes sparkling with excitement at the prospect of a fight.

"I don't want to fight with a girl," he said, considerably astonished at vigorous resistance where he had expected timid submission.

"You're afraid!" said Tom, triumphantly.

"No, I'm not," said George, backing out all the while; "I don't want to hurt you."

"You can't do it," said Tom; "I can lick you any day."

"How could you do it?" asked Fanny, as the dreaded bully slunk away. "How brave you are, Jenny! I'm awful afraid of him."

"You needn't be," said Tom, taking her books. "I've licked boys bigger'n him. I can lick him, and he knows it."

She was right. The story got about, and George Griffiths was so laughed at, for being vanquished by a girl, that he was very careful in future whom he attempted to bully.

CHAPTER XIII
GRANNY IS COMPELLED TO EARN HER OWN LIVING.

Leaving Tom in her new home, we return to Mrs. Walsh, which was the proper designation of the old woman whom she called granny. Though Tom had escaped from her clutches, granny had no idea that she intended to stay away permanently. She did not consider that all the advantages of the connection between them had been on her side, and that Tom had only had the privilege of supporting them both. If she had not carried matters so far our heroine would have been satisfied to remain; but now she had fairly broken away, and would never come back unless brought by force.

When six o'clock came granny began to wonder why Tom did not come back. She usually returned earlier, with whatever money she had managed to obtain.

"She's afraid of a lickin'," thought granny. "She'll get a wuss one if she stays away."

An hour passed, and granny became hungry; but unfortunately she was penniless, and had nothing in the room except a crust of hard bread which she intended for Tom's supper. Hunger compelled her to eat this herself, though it was not much to her taste. Every moment's additional delay irritated her the more with the rebellious Tom.

"I wish I had her here," soliloquized granny, spitefully.

When it was half-past seven granny resolved to go out and hunt her up. She might be on the sidewalk outside playing. Perhaps—but this was too daring for belief—she might be spending her afternoon's earnings on another square meal.

Granny went downstairs, and through the archway into the street. There were plenty of children, living in neighboring tenement houses, gathered in groups or playing about, but no Tom was visible.

"Have you seen anything of my gal, Micky Murphy?" asked granny of a boy whom she had often seen with Tom.

"No," said Micky. "I haven't seen her."

"Haven't any of you seen her?" demanded Mrs. Walsh, making the question a general one.

"I seen her sellin' papers," said one boy.

"When was that?" asked granny, eagerly.

"'Bout four o'clock."

"Where was she?"

"Greenwich Street."

This was a clue at least, but a faint one. Tom had been seen at four o'clock, and now it was nearly eight. Long before this she must have sold her papers, and the unpleasant conviction dawned upon granny that she must have spent her earnings upon herself.

"If I could only get hold of her!" muttered granny, vengefully.

She went as far as the City Hall, and followed along down by the Park fence, looking about her in all directions, in the hope that she might espy Tom. But the latter was at this time engaging lodgings for the night, as we know, and in no danger of being caught.

Unwilling to give up the pursuit, Mrs. Walsh wandered about for an hour or more, occasionally resting on one of the seats in the City Hall Park, till the unwonted exertion began to weary her, and she realized that she was not likely to encounter Tom.

There was one chance left. Tom might have got home while she had been in search of her. Spurred by this hope, Mrs. Walsh hurried home, and mounted to her lofty room. But it was as desolate as when she left it. It was quite clear that Tom did not mean to come back that night. This was provoking; but granny still was confident that she would return in the course of the next day. So she threw herself on the bed,—not without some silent imprecations upon her rebellious charge,—and slept till morning.

Morning brought her a new realization of her loss. She found her situation by no means an agreeable one. Her appetite was excellent, but she was without food or money to buy a supply. It was certainly provoking to think that she must look out for herself. However, granny was equal to the occasion. She did not propose to work for a living, but decided that she would throw herself upon charity. To begin with, she obtained some breakfast of a poor but charitable neighbor, and then started on a walk up town. It was not till she got as far as Fourteenth Street that she commenced her round of visits.

The first house at which she stopped was an English basement house. Granny rang the basement bell.

"Is your mistress at home?" she asked.

"Yes; what's wanted?"

"I'm a poor widder," whined granny, in a lugubrious voice, "with five small children. We haven't got a bit of food in the house. Can't you give me a few pennies?"

"I'll speak to the missis, but I don't think she'll give any money."

She went upstairs, and soon returned.

"She won't give you any money, but here's a loaf of bread."

Mrs. Walsh would much have preferred a small sum of money, but muttered her thanks, and dropped the loaf into a bag she had brought with her.

She went on to the next block, and intercepted a gentleman just starting down town to his business.

"I'm a poor widder," she said, repeating her whine; "will you give me a few pennies? and may the Lord bless you!"

"Why don't you work?" asked the gentleman, brusquely.

"I'm too old and feeble," she answered, bending over to assume the appearance of infirmity. This did not escape the attention of the gentleman, who answered unceremoniously, "You're a humbug! You won't get anything from me! If I had my way, I'd have you arrested and locked up."

Granny trembled with passion, but did not think it politic to give vent to her fury.

Her next application was more successful, twenty-five cents being sent to the door by a compassionate lady, who never doubted the story of the five little children suffering at home for want of food.

Granny's eyes sparkled with joy as she hastily clutched the money. With it she could buy drink and tobacco, while food was not an object of barter.

"The missis wants to know where you live," said the servant.

Mrs. Walsh gave a wrong address, not caring to receive charitable callers, who would inevitably find out that her story was a false one, and her children mythical.

At the next house she got no money; but on declaring that she had eaten nothing for twenty-four hours, was invited into the kitchen, where she was offered a chair, and a plate of meat and bread was placed before her. This invitation was rather an embarrassing one; for, thanks to her charitable neighbor, granny had eaten quite a hearty breakfast not long before. But, having declared that she had not tasted food for twenty-four hours, she was compelled to keep up appearances, and eat what was set before her. It was very hard work, and attracted the attention of the servants, who had supposed her half famished.

"You don't seem very hungry," said Annie, the cook.

"It's because I'm faint-like," muttered granny. At this moment her bag, containing the loaf of bread, tumbled on the floor.

"What's that?" asked the cook, suspiciously.

"It's some bread I'm goin' to carry home to the childers," said Mrs. Walsh, a little confused. "They was crying for something to ate when I come away."

"Then you'd better take it home as soon as you can," said Annie, surveying the old woman with some suspicion.

Granny was forced to leave something on her plate, nature refusing the double burden she sought to impose upon it, and went out with an uncomfortable sense of fulness. Resuming her rounds, she was repulsed at some places, at others referred to this or that charitable society, but in the end succeeded in raising twenty-five cents more in money. Fifty cents, a loaf of bread, and a little cold meat represented her gains of the morning, and with these she felt tolerably well satisfied. She had been compelled to walk up town, but now she had money and could afford to ride. She entered a Sixth Avenue car, therefore, and in half an hour or thereabouts reached the Astor House. She walked through the Park, looking about her carefully, in the hope of seeing Tom, who would certainly have fared badly if she had fallen into the clutches of the angry old woman. But Tom was nowhere visible.

So granny plodded home, and, mounting to her room, laid away the bread and meat, and, throwing herself upon the bed, indulged in a pipe. Tom was not at home, and granny began to have apprehensions that she meant to stay away longer than she had at first supposed.

"But I'll come across her some day," said granny, vindictively. "When I do I'll break every bone in her body."

The old woman lay on the bed two or three hours, and then went out, with the double purpose of investing a part of her funds in a glass of something strong, and in the hope that she might fall in with Tom. Notwithstanding the desire of vengeance, she missed her. She had not the slightest affection for the young girl who had been so long her charge, but she was used to her companionship. It seemed lonely without her. Besides, granny had one of those uncomfortable dispositions that feel lost without some one to scold and tyrannize over, and, although Tom had not been so yielding and submissive as many girls would have been under the same circumstances, Mrs. Walsh had had the satisfaction of beating her occasionally, and naturally longed for the presence of her customary victim.

So, after making the purchase she intended, granny made another visit to the Park and Printing House Square, and inspected eagerly the crowds of street children who haunt those localities as paper-venders, peddlers, and boot-blacks. But Tom, as we know, was by this time an inmate of Mrs. Merton's boarding-house,—the home found for her by her friend, the sea-captain. This was quite out of Mrs. Walsh's beat. She had not anticipated any such contingency, but supposed that Tom would be forced to earn her living by some of those street trades by means of which so many children are kept from starvation. It did not enter her calculations that, so soon after parting from her, Tom had also ceased to be a street Arab, and obtained a respectable home. Of course, therefore, disappointment was again her portion, and she was forced to return home and go to bed without the exquisite satisfaction of "breaking every bone in Tom's body."

Granny felt that she was ill-used, and that Tom was a monster of ingratitude; but on that subject there may, perhaps, be a difference of opinion.

CHAPTER XIV
TOM IS CAPTURED BY THE ENEMY.

We pass over two months, in which nothing of striking interest occurred to our heroine, or her affectionate relative, who continued to mourn her loss with more of anger than of sorrow. My readers may be interested to know how far Tom has improved in this interval. I am glad to say that she has considerably changed for the better, and is rather less of an Arab than when she entered the house. Still Mrs. Merton, on more than one occasion, had assured her intimate friend and gossip, Miss Betsy Perkins, that Tom was "a great trial," and nothing but her promise to her brother induced her to keep her.

Tom was, however, very quick and smart. She learned with great rapidity, when she chose, and was able to be of considerable service in the house before and after school. To be sure she was always getting into hot water, and from time to time indulged in impish freaks, which betrayed her street-training. At school, however, she learned very rapidly, and had already been promoted into a class higher than that which she entered. If there was one thing that Tom was ashamed of, it was to find herself the largest and oldest girl in her class. She was ambitious to stand as well as other girls of her own age, and, with this object in view, studied with characteristic energy, and as a consequence improved rapidly.

She did not get along very well with Mary Merton. Mary was languid and affected, and looked down scornfully upon her mother's hired girl, as she called her; though, as we know, money was paid for Tom's board. Tom did not care much for her taunts, being able to give as good as she sent; but there was one subject on which Mary had it in her power to annoy her. This was about her defective education.

"You don't know any more than a girl of eight," said Mary, contemptuously.

"I haven't been to school all my life as you have," said Tom.

"I know that," said Mary. "You were nothing but a beggar, or rag-picker, or something of that kind. I don't see what made my uncle take you out of the street. That was the best place for you."

"I wish you had to live with granny for a month," retorted Tom. "It would do you good to get a lickin' now and then."

"Your grandmother must have been a very low person," said Mary, disdainfully.

"That's where you're right," said Tom, whose affection for granny was not very great.

"I'm glad I haven't such a grandmother. I should be ashamed of it."

"She wasn't my grandmother. She only called herself so," said Tom.

"I've no doubt she was," said Mary, "and that you are just like her."

"Say that again, and I'll punch your head," said Tom, belligerently.

As Mary knew that Tom was quite capable of doing what she threatened, she prudently desisted, but instead taunted her once more with her ignorance.

"Never mind," said Tom, "wait a while and I'll catch up with you."

Mary laughed a spiteful little laugh.

"Hear her talk!" she said. "Why, I've been ever so far in English; besides, I am studying French."

"Can't I study French too?"

"That would be a great joke for a common street girl to study French! You'll be playing the piano next."

"Why not?" asked Tom, undauntedly.

"Maybe your granny, as you call her, had a piano."

"Perhaps she did," said Tom; "but it was to the blacksmith's to be mended, so I never saw it."

Tom was not in the least sensitive on the subject of granny, and however severe reflections might be indulged in upon granny's character and position, she bore them with equanimity, not feeling any particular interest in the old woman.

Still she did occasionally feel a degree of curiosity as to how granny was getting along in her absence. She enjoyed the thought that Mrs. Walsh, no longer being able to rely upon her, would be compelled to forage for herself.

"I wonder what she'll do," thought Tom. "She's such a lazy old woman that I think she'll go round beggin'. Work don't agree with her constitution."

It so happened that granny, though in her new vocation she made frequent excursions up town, had never fallen in with Tom. This was partly because Tom spent the hours from nine to two in school, and it was at this time that granny always went on her rounds. But one Saturday forenoon Tom was sent on an errand some half a mile distant. As she was passing through Eighteenth Street her attention was drawn to a tall, ill-dressed figure a few feet in advance of her. Though only her back was visible, Tom remembered something peculiar in granny's walk.

"That's granny," soliloquized Tom, in excitement; "she's out beggin', I'll bet a hat."

The old woman carried a basket in one hand, for the reception of cold victuals, for, though she preferred money, provisions were also acceptable, and she had learned from experience that there were some who refrained from giving money on principle, but would not refuse food.

Tom was not anxious to fall into the old woman's clutches. Still she felt like following her up, and hearing what she had to say.

She had not long to wait.

Granny turned into the area of an English basement house, and rang the basement bell.

Tom paused, and leaned her back against the railing, in such a position that she could hear what passed.

A servant answered the bell.

"What do you want?" she asked, not very ceremoniously.

"I'm a poor widder," whined granny, "with five small children. They haven't had anything to eat since yesterday. Can't you give me something? and may the Lord bless you!"

"She knows how to lie," thought Tom. "So she's got five small children!"

"You're pretty old to have five small children," said the servant, suspiciously.

"I aint so old as I look," said Mrs. Walsh. "It's bein' poor and destitoot that makes me look old before my time."

"Where's your husband?"

"He's dead," said granny. "He treated me bad; he used to drink, and then bate me and the children."

"You look as if you drank, yourself."

"I'd scorn the action," said granny, virtuously. "I never could bear whiskey."

"Aint she doin' it up brown?" thought Tom. "Haven't I seen her pourin' it down though?"

"Give me your basket," said the servant.

"Can't you give me some money," whined granny, "to help pay the rint?"

"We never give money," said the servant.

She went into the kitchen, and shortly returned with some cold meat and bread. Granny opened it to see what it contained.

"Haven't you got any cold chicken?" she asked, rather dissatisfied.

"She's got cheek," thought Tom.

"If you're not satisfied with what you've got, you needn't come again."

"Yes," said granny, "I'm satisfied; but my little girl is sick, and can't bear anything but chicken, or maybe turkey."

"Then you must ask for it somewhere else," said the servant. "We haven't got any for you here."

Having obtained all she was likely to get, granny prepared to go.

Tom felt that she, too, must start, for there might be danger of identification. To be sure she was now well-dressed,—quite as well as the average of girls of her age. The cap and jacket, indeed all that had made her old name of "Tattered Tom" appropriate, had disappeared, and she was very different in appearance from the young Arab whom we became acquainted with in the first chapter. In other respects, as we know, Tom had not altered quite so much. There was considerable of the Arab about her still, though there was a prospect of her eventually becoming entirely tamed.

Granny just glanced at the young girl, whose back only was visible to her, but never thought of identifying her with her lost grand-daughter. Sometimes, however, she had obtained money from compassionate school-girls, and it struck her that there might be a chance in this quarter.

She advanced, and tapped Tom on the shoulder.

"Little gal," she dolefully said, "I'm a poor widder with five small children. Can't you give me a few pennies? and may the Lord reward you!"

Tom was a little startled, but quite amused, by this application from granny. She knew there was danger in answering; but there was a fascination about danger, and she thought that, even if identified, she could make her escape.

"Where do you live?" she asked, trying to disguise her voice, and looking down.

"No. Bleecker Street," said granny, at random, intentionally giving the wrong address.

"I'll get my aunt to come round to-morrow and see you," said Tom.

"Give me a few pennies now," persisted granny, "to buy some bread for my children."

"How many have you got?"

"Five."

It was very imprudent, but Tom obeyed an irresistible impulse, and said, "Isn't one of them named Tom?" and she looked up in her old way.

Granny bent over eagerly, and looked in her face. She had noticed something familiar in the voice, but the dress had prevented her from suspecting anything. Now it flashed upon her that the rebellious Tom was in her clutches.

"So it's you, is it?" she said, with grim delight, clutching Tom by the arm. "I've found you at last, you trollop! Come along with me! I'll break every bone in your body!"

Tom saw that she had incautiously incurred a great peril; but she had no idea of being dragged away unresisting. She was quick-witted, and saw that, if she chose to deny all knowledge of the old woman, granny would find it hard to substantiate her claims.

"Stop that, old woman!" she said, without the least appearance of fear. "If you don't let go, I'll have you arrested!"

"You will, will you?" exclaimed granny, giving her a shake viciously. "We'll see about that. Where'd you get all them good clothes from? Come along home."

"Let me alone!" said Tom. "You've got nothing to do with me."

"Got nothing to do with you? Aint I your granny?"

"You must be crazy," said Tom, coolly. "My grandmother don't go round the streets, begging for cold victuals."

"Do you mean to say I'm not your granny?" demanded the old woman, astounded.

"I don't know what you mean," said Tom, coolly. "You'd better go home to your five small children in Bleecker Street."

"O you trollop!" muttered granny, giving her a violent shaking; which reminded Tom of old times in not the most agreeable manner.

"Come, old woman, that's played out!" said Tom. "You'd better stop that."

"You're my gal, and I've a right to lick you," said Mrs. Walsh.

"I've got nothing to do with you."

"Come along!" said granny, attempting to drag Tom with her.

But Tom made a vigorous resistance, and granny began to fear that she had undertaken rather a hard task. The distance from Eighteenth Street to the tenement house which she called home was two miles, probably, and it would not be very easy to drag Tom that distance against her will. A ride in the horse-cars was impracticable, since she had no money with her.

The struggle was still going on, when Tom all at once espied a policeman coming around the corner. She did not hesitate to take advantage of his opportune appearance.

"Help! Police!" exclaimed Tom, in a loud voice.

This sudden appeal startled granny, whose associations with the police were not of the most agreeable nature, and she nearly released her hold. She glared at Tom in speechless rage, foreseeing that trouble was coming.

"What's the matter?" asked the officer, coming up, and regarding the two attentively.

"I think this woman must be crazy," said Tom. "She came up and asked me for a few pennies, and then grabbed me by the arm, saying she was my granny. She is trying to drag me home with her."

"What have you to say to this?" demanded the policeman.

"She's my gal," said granny, doggedly.

"You hear her," said Tom. "Do I look as if I belonged to her? She's a common beggar."

"O you ungrateful trollop!" shrieked granny, tightening her grip.

"She hurts me," said Tom. "Won't you make her let go?"

"Let her go!" said the policeman, authoritatively.

"But she's my gal."

"Let go, I tell you!" and granny was forced to obey. "Now where do you live?"

" Bleecker Street."
"You said it was just now," said Tom, "and that you had five small children. Was I one of them?"

Granny was cornered. She was afraid that Bleecker Street might be visited, and her imposture discovered. It was hard to give up Tom, and so have the girl, whom she now hated intensely, triumph over her. She would make one more attempt.

"She's my gal. She run away from me two months ago."

"If you've got five small children at home, and have to beg for a living," said the officer, who did not believe a word of her story, "you have all you can take care of. She's better off where she is."

"Can't I take her home, then?" asked granny, angrily.

"You had better go away quietly," said the policeman, "or I must take you to the station-house."

Mrs. Walsh, compelled to abandon her designs upon Tom, moved off slowly. She had got but a few steps, when Tom called out to her, "Give my love to your five small children, granny!"

The old woman, by way of reply, turned and shook her fist menacingly at Tom, but the latter only laughed and went on her way.

"Aint she mad, though!" soliloquized Tom. "She'd lick me awful if she only got a chance. I'm glad I don't live with her. Now I get square meals every day. I'd like to see granny's five small children;" and Tom laughed heartily at what she thought a smart imposture. That Tom should be very conscientious on the subject of truth could hardly be expected. A street education, and such guardianship as she had received from granny, were not likely to make her a model; but Tom is more favorably situated now, and we may hope for gradual improvement.

CHAPTER XV
GRANNY READS SOMETHING TO HER ADVANTAGE.
After her unsuccessful attempt to gain possession of Tom, granny returned home, not only angry but despondent. She had been deeply incensed at Tom's triumph over her. Besides, she was tired of earning her own living, if begging from door to door can properly be called earning one's living. At any rate it required

exertion, and to this Mrs. Walsh was naturally indisposed. She sighed as she thought of the years when she could stay quietly at home, and send out Tom to beg or earn money for her. She would like, since Tom was not likely to return, to adopt some boy or girl of suitable age, upon whom she could throw the burden of the common support. But such were not easy to be met with, and Mrs. Walsh was dimly aware that no sane child would voluntarily select her as a guardian.

So granny, in rather low spirits, sought her elevated room, and threw herself upon the bed to sleep off her fatigue.

On awaking, granny seated herself at the window, and picked up mechanically the advertising sheet of the "Herald," in which a loaf of bread had been wrapped that had been given to her the day previous. It was seldom that Mrs. Walsh indulged in reading, not possessing very marked literary tastes; but to-day she was seized with an idle impulse, which she obeyed, without anticipating that she would see anything that concerned her.

In glancing through the advertisements under the head "Personal," her attention was drawn to the following:—

/# "If Margaret Walsh, who left Philadelphia in the year , will call at No. — Wall Street, Room , she will hear of something to her advantage." #/

"Why, that's me!" exclaimed granny, letting the paper fall from her lap in surprise. "It's my name, and I left Philadelphy that year. I wonder what it's about. Maybe it's about Tom."

There were circumstances which led Mrs. Walsh to think it by no means improbable that the inquiries to be made were about Tom, and this made her regret more keenly that she had lost her.

"If it is," she soliloquized, "I'll get hold of her somehow."

There was one part of the advertisement which particularly interested granny,—that in which it was suggested that she would hear something to her advantage. If there was any money to be made, granny was entirely willing to make it. Considering the unpromising state of her prospects, she felt that it was a piece of extraordinary good luck.

Looking at the date of the paper, she found that it was a fortnight old, and was troubled by the thought that it might be too late. At any rate no time was to be lost. So, in spite of the fatigue of her morning expedition, she put on her old cloak and bonnet, and, descending the stairs, sallied out into the street. She made her way down Nassau Street to Wall, and, carefully looking about her, found without difficulty the number mentioned in the advertisement. It was a large building, containing a considerable number of offices. No. was on the third floor. On the door was a tin sign bearing the name:—

"EUGENE SELDEN,
Attorney and Counsellor."

Mrs. Walsh knocked at the door; but there was no response. She knocked again, after a while, and then tried the door. But it was locked.

"The office closes at three, ma'am," said a young man, passing by. "You will have to wait till to-morrow."

Mrs. Walsh was disappointed, being very anxious to ascertain what advantage she was likely to receive. She presented herself the next morning at nine, only to find herself too early. At last she found the lawyer in. He looked up from his desk as she entered.

"Have you business with me?" he asked.

"Are you the man that advertised for Margaret Walsh?" asked granny.

"Yes," said Mr. Selden, laying down his pen, and regarding her with interest. "Are you she?"

"Yes, your honor," said granny, thinking her extra politeness might increase the advantage promised.

"Did you ever live in Philadelphia?"

"Yes, your honor."

"Were you in service?"

Mrs. Walsh answered in the affirmative.

"In what family?"

"In the family of Mrs. Lindsay."

"What made you leave her?" asked the lawyer, fixing his eyes searchingly upon Margaret.

Granny looked a little uneasy.

"I got tired of staying there," she said.

"When you left Philadelphia, did you come to New York?"

"Yes, your honor."

"Did you know that Mrs. Lindsay's only child disappeared at the time you left the house?" inquired the lawyer.

"If I tell the truth will it harm me?" asked granny, uneasily.

"No; but if you conceal the truth it may."

"Then I took the child with me."

"What motive had you for doing this wicked thing? Do you know that Mrs. Lindsay nearly broke her heart at the loss of the child?"

"I was mad with her," said granny, "that's one reason."

"Then there was another reason?"

"Yes, your honor."

"What was it?"

"Young Mr. Lindsay hired me to do it. He offered me a thousand dollars."

"Are you ready to swear this?"

"Yes," said granny. "I hope you'll pay me handsome for tellin'," she added. "I'm a poor—woman," she was on the point of saying "widder with five small children;" but it occurred to her that this would injure her in the present instance.

"You shall receive a suitable reward when the child is restored. It is living, I suppose?"

"Yes," said granny.

"With you?"

"No, your honor. She ran away two months ago; but I saw her this morning."

"Why should she run away? Didn't you treat her well?"

"Like as if she was my own child," said granny. "I've often and often gone without anything to eat, so that Tom might have enough. I took great care of her, your honor, and would have brought her up as a leddy if I hadn't been so poor."

"I thought it was a girl."

"So it was, your honor."

"Then why do you call her Tom?"

"'Cause she was more like a boy than a gal,—as sassy a child as I ever see."

"So you have lost her?"

"Yes, your honor. She ran away from me two months since."

"But you said you saw her yesterday. Why did you not take her back?"

"She wouldn't come. She told the policeman she didn't know me,—me that have took care of her since she was a little gal,—the ungrateful hussy!"

Granny's pathos, it will be perceived, terminated in anger.

The lawyer looked thoughtful.

"The child must be got back," he said. "It is only recently that her mother ascertained the treachery by which she was taken from her, and now she is most anxious to recover her. If you will bring her to me, you shall have a suitable reward."

"How much?" asked granny, with a cunning look.

"I cannot promise in advance, but it will certainly be two hundred dollars,—perhaps more. Mrs. Lindsay will be generous."

The old woman's eyes sparkled. Such a sum promised an unlimited amount of whiskey for a considerable time. The only disagreeable feature in the case was that Tom would benefit by the restoration, since she would obtain a comfortable home, and a parent whose ideas of the parental relation differed somewhat from those of Mrs. Walsh. Still, two hundred dollars were worth the winning, and granny determined to win them. She suggested, however, that, in order to secure the co-operation of the police, she needed to be more respectably dressed; otherwise her claim would be scouted, provided Tom undertook to deny it.

This appeared reasonable, and as the lawyer had authority to incur any expense that he might consider likely to further the successful prosecution of the search, he sent out some one, in whom he had confidence, to purchase a respectable outfit for Mrs. Walsh. He further agreed to allow her three dollars a week for the present, that she might be able to devote all her time to hunting up Tom. This arrangement was very satisfactory to Mrs. Walsh, who felt like a lady in easy circumstances. Her return to the tenement house, in her greatly improved dress, created quite a sensation. She did not deign to enlighten her neighbors upon the cause of her improved fortunes, but dropped hints that she had come into a legacy.

From this time Mrs. Walsh began to frequent the up-town streets, particularly Eighteenth Street, where she had before encountered Tom. But as she still continued to make her rounds in the morning, it was many days before she caught a glimpse of the object of her search. As her expenses were paid in the mean time, she waited patiently, though she anticipated with no little pleasure the moment which should place Tom in her power. She resolved, before restoring her to her mother, to inflict upon her late ward a suitable punishment for her rebellion and flight, for which granny was not likely ever to forgive her.

"I'll give her something to remember me by," muttered granny. "See if I don't!"

CHAPTER XVI
TOM IN TROUBLE.

The reader has already obtained some idea of the character of Mary Merton. She was weak, vain, affected, and fond of dress. There was not likely to be much love lost between her and Tom, who was in all respects her opposite. Whatever might have been the defects of her street education, it had at all events secured Tom from such faults as these.

Mary sought the society of such of her companions as were wealthy or fashionable, and was anxious to emulate them in dress. But unfortunately her mother's income was limited, and she could not gratify her tastes. She was continually teasing Mrs. Merton for this and that article of finery; but, though her mother spent more for her than she could well afford, she was obliged in many cases to disappoint her. So it happened that Mary was led into temptation.

One morning she was going downstairs on her way to school. The door of Mr. Holland's room (who occupied the second floor front) chanced to be open. It occurred to Mary that the large mirror in this room would enable her to survey her figure to advantage, and, being fond of looking in the glass, she entered.

After satisfactorily accomplishing the object of her visit, Mary, in glancing about, caught sight of a pocket-book on the bureau. Curiosity led her to approach and open it. It proved to contain four five-dollar bills and a small amount of change.

"I wish the money was mine," said Mary to herself.

There was a particular object for which she wanted it. Two of her companions had handsome gold pencils, which they wore suspended by a cord around their necks. Mary had teased her mother to buy her one, but Mrs. Merton had turned a deaf ear to her request. Finally she had given up asking, finding that it would be of no avail.

"If I only had this money, or half of it," thought Mary, "I could buy a pencil for myself, and tell mother it was given me by one of my friends."

The temptation, to a vain girl like Mary, was a strong one.

"Shall I take it?" she thought.

The dishonesty of the act did not so much deter her as the fear of detection. But the idea unluckily suggested itself that Tom would be far more likely to be suspected than she.

"Mr. Holland is rich," she said to herself; "he won't feel the loss."

She held the pocket-book irresolutely in her hand, uncertain whether to take a part of the contents or the whole. Finally she opened it, drew out the bills, amounting to twenty dollars, hastily thrust them into her pocket, and, replacing the pocket-book on the bureau, went downstairs.

She met her mother in the lower hall.

"I am afraid you will be late to school, Mary," she said.

"I couldn't find my shoes for a long time," said Mary, flushing a little at the thought of the money in her pocket.

Mr. Holland's room had already been attended to, and was not again entered until half-past five in the afternoon, when Mr. Holland, who was a clerk in a down-town office, returned home.

He had missed the pocket-book shortly after leaving the house in the morning, but, being expected at the office at a certain hour, had not been able to return for it. He had borrowed money of a fellow-clerk to pay for his lunch.

As he entered the room, he saw his pocket-book lying on the bureau.

"There it is, all safe," he said to himself, quite relieved; for, though in receipt of a handsome salary, no one would care to lose twenty dollars.

He was about to put the pocket-book into his pocket unexamined, when it occurred to him to open it, and make sure that the contents were untouched. He was startled on finding less than a dollar, where he distinctly remembered that there had been nearly twenty-one dollars.

"Some one has taken it," he said to himself. "I must see Mrs. Merton about this."

He did not get an opportunity of speaking to the landlady until after dinner, when he called her aside, and told her of his loss.

"Are you quite sure, Mr. Holland," she asked, considerably disturbed, "there were twenty dollars in the pocket-book?"

"Yes, Mrs. Merton. I remember distinctly having counted the money this morning, before laying it on the bureau. It must have been taken by some one in the house. Now, who was likely to enter the room? Which of your servants makes the bed?"

"It was Jenny," said Mrs. Merton, with a sudden conviction that Tom was the guilty party.

"What, that bright little girl that I have seen about the house?"

"Yes, Mr. Holland, I am afraid it is she," said Mrs. Merton, shaking her head. "She is not exactly a servant, but a child whom my brother took out of the streets, and induced me to take charge of while he is away. She has been very ill-trained, and I am not surprised to find her dishonest. More than once I have regretted taking charge of her."

"I am sorry," said Mr. Holland. "I have noticed that she is rather different from most girls. I wish I had not exposed her to the temptation."

"She must give up the money, or I won't keep her in the house," said Mrs. Merton, who had become indignant at Tom's ingratitude, as she considered it. "My brother can't expect me to harbor a thief in the house, even for his sake. It would ruin the reputation of my house if such a thing happened again."

"She will probably give it back when she finds herself detected," said Mr. Holland.

"I will tax her with it at once," said the landlady. "Stay here, Mr. Holland, and I will call her."

Tom was called in. She looked from one to the other, and something in the expression of each led her to see that she was to be blamed for something, though what she could not conceive.

"Jane," said Mrs. Merton, sternly, "my brother will be very much grieved when he learns how badly you have behaved to-day."

"What have I been doing?" asked Tom, looking up with a fearless glance, not by any means like a girl conscious of theft.

"You have taken twenty dollars belonging to Mr. Holland."

"Who says I did it?" demanded Tom.

"It is useless to deny it. You cleared up his room this morning. His pocket-book was on the bureau."

"I know it was," said Tom. "I saw it there."

"You opened it, and took out twenty dollars."

"No, I didn't," said Tom. "I didn't touch it."

"Do not add falsehood to theft. You must have done it. There was no one else likely to do it."

"Wasn't the door unlocked all day?" demanded Tom. "Why couldn't some one else go in and take it as well as I?"

"I feel sure it was you."

"Why?" asked Tom, her eyes beginning to flash indignantly.

"I have no doubt you have stolen before. My brother took you from the street. You were brought up by a bad old woman, as you say yourself. I ought not to be surprised at your yielding to temptation. If you will restore the money to Mr. Holland, and promise not to steal again, I will overlook your offence, and allow you to remain in the house, since it was my brother's wish."

"Mrs. Merton," said Tom, proudly, "I didn't take the money, and I can't give it back. I might have stolen when I lived with granny, for I didn't get enough to eat half the time, but I wouldn't do it now."

"That sounds well," said Mrs. Merton; "but somebody must have taken the money."

"I don't care who took it," said Tom, "I didn't."

"You are more likely to have taken it than any one else."

"You may search me if you want to," said Tom, proudly.

"Perhaps she didn't take it," said Mr. Holland, upon whom Tom's fearless bearing had made an impression.

"I will inquire if any of the servants went into your room," said Mrs. Merton. "If not, I must conclude that Jane took it."

Inquiry was made, but it appeared evident that no servant had entered the room. Tom had made the bed and attended to the chamber-work alone. Mrs. Merton was therefore confirmed in her suspicions. She summoned Tom once more, and offered to forgive her if she would make confession and restitution.

"I didn't steal the money," said Tom, indignantly. "I've told you that before."

"Unless you give it up, I cannot consent to have you remain longer in my house."

"All right!" said Tom, defiantly. "I don't want to stay if that's what you think of me."

She turned and left Mrs. Merton. Five minutes later she was in the street, going she knew not whither. She was so angry at the unfounded suspicions which had been cast upon her, that she felt glad to go. But after a while she began to think of the sudden change in her fortunes. For three months she had possessed a comfortable home, been well fed and lodged, and had been rapidly making up the deficiencies in her education. She had really tried to soften the roughness and abruptness of her manners, and become a good girl, hoping to win the approbation of her good friend, the captain, when he should return from his voyage. Now it was all over. She had lost her home, and must again wander about with no home but the inhospitable street.

"It isn't my fault," thought Tom, with a sigh. "I couldn't give back the money when I didn't take it."

CHAPTER XVII
THE GOLD PENCIL.

Mrs. Merton was taken by surprise when she found that Tom had actually gone. Her conviction remained unshaken that she had stolen Mr. Holland's money, and she considered that she had been forbearing in not causing her arrest.

"Your uncle cannot blame me," she said to Mary, "for sending her away. He cannot expect me to keep a thief in my house."

"To be sure not," said Mary, promptly. "I am glad she has gone. You couldn't expect much from a girl that was brought up in the streets."

"That is true. I don't see, for my part, what your uncle saw in her."

"Nor I. She's a rude, hateful thing."

"She denied taking the money."

"Of course," said Mary. "She wouldn't mind lying any more than stealing."

Mary felt very much relieved at the way things had turned out. After taking the money, she had become frightened lest in some way suspicion might be directed towards herself. As she had hoped, her fault had been laid to Tom, and now she felt comparatively safe. She had not yet dared to use the money, but thought she might venture to do so soon.

She went up to her bedroom, and, after locking the door, opened her trunk. The four five-dollar bills were carefully laid away in one corner, underneath a pile of clothes. Mary counted them over with an air of satisfaction. Her conscience did not trouble her much as long as the fear of detection was removed.

"Mr. Holland won't miss the money," she thought, "and everybody'll think Jane took it."

The thought of her own meanness in depriving Tom of a good home, and sending her out into the street without shelter or money, never suggested itself to the selfish girl. She felt glad to be rid of her, and did not trouble herself about any discomforts or privations that she might experience.

Three days later Mary felt that she might venture to buy the pencil which she had so long coveted. Tom's disappearance was accepted by all in the house as a confirmation of the charge of theft, and no one else was likely to be suspected. Not knowing how much the pencil was likely to cost, Mary took the entire twenty dollars with her. She stopped on her way from school at a jewelry store only a few blocks distant from her mother's house. She was unwise in not going farther away, since this increased the chances of her detection.

"Let me look at your gold pencils," she asked, with an air of importance.

The salesman produced a variety of pencils, varying in price.

Mary finally made choice of one that cost twelve dollars.

She paid over the money with much satisfaction, for the pencil was larger and handsomer than those belonging to her companions, which had excited her envy. She also bought a silk chain, to which she attached it, and then hung it round her neck.

Though Mary was not aware of it, her entrance into the jewelry store had been remarked by Mrs. Carver, a neighbor and acquaintance of her mother's. Mrs. Carver, like some others of her sex, was gifted with curiosity, and wondered considerably what errand had carried Mary into the jeweller's.

Bent upon finding out, she entered the store and approached the counter.

"What did that young girl buy?" she asked.

"You mean that one who just went out?"

"Yes."

"A gold pencil-case."

"Indeed," said Mrs. Carver, looking surprised. "How expensive a pencil did she buy?"

"She paid twelve dollars."

"Will you show me one like it?"

A pencil, precisely similar, was shown Mrs. Carver, the clerk supposing she wished to purchase. But she had obtained all the information she desired.

"I won't decide to-day," she said. "I will come in again."

"There's some mystery about this," said Mrs. Carver to herself. "I wonder where Mary got so much money; surely, her mother could not have given it to her. If she did, all I have to say is, that she is very extravagant for a woman that keeps boarders for a living."

Mrs. Carver was one of those women who feel a very strong interest in the business of others. The friends with whom she was most intimate were most likely to incur her criticism. In the present instance she was determined to fathom the mystery of the gold pencil.

Mary went home with her treasure. Of course she knew that its possession would excite surprise, and she had a story prepared to account for it. She felt a little nervous, but had little doubt that her account would be believed.

As she anticipated, the pencil at once attracted her mother's attention.

"Whose pencil is that, Mary?" she asked.

"Mine, mother."

"Yours? Where did you get it?" inquired her mother, in surprise.

"Sue Cameron gave it to me. She's my bosom friend, you know."

"Let me see it. It isn't gold—is it?"

"Yes, it's solid gold," said Mary, complacently.

"But I don't understand her giving you so expensive a present. It must have cost a good deal."

"So it did. Sue said it cost twelve dollars."

"Then how came she to give it to you?"

"Oh, her father's awful rich! Besides, Sue has had another pencil given to her, and she didn't want but one; so she gave me this."

"It looks as if it were new."

"Yes, she has had it only a short time."

"When did she give it to you?"

"This morning. She promised it to me a week ago," said Mary, in a matter-of-fact manner which quite deceived her mother.

"She has certainly been very kind to you. She must like you very much."

"Yes, she does. She likes me better than any of the other girls."

"Why don't you invite her to come and see you? You ought to be polite to her, since she is so kind."

This suggestion was by no means pleasing to Mary. In the first place Sue Cameron was by no means the intimate friend she represented, and in the next, if she called and Mrs. Merton referred to the gift, it would at once let the cat out of the bag, and Mary would be in trouble. Therefore she said, "I'll invite her, mother, but I don't think she'll come."

"Why not?"

"She lives away up on Fifth Avenue, and is not allowed to make visits without some one of the family. The Camerons are very rich, you know, and stuck up. Only Sue is not."

"You'd better invite her, however, Mary, since she is such a friend of yours."

"Yes, I will, only you must not be surprised if she does not come."

The next afternoon Mrs. Carver dropped in for a call. While she was talking with Mrs. Merton, Mary came into the room. Her gold pencil was ostentatiously displayed.

"How do you do, Mary?" said the visitor. "What a handsome pencil-case you have!"

"One of her school friends gave it to her," explained Mrs. Merton.

"Indeed!" returned Mrs. Carver, with an emphasis which bespoke surprise.

"Yes," continued Mrs. Merton, unconsciously. "It was a Miss Cameron, whose father lives on Fifth Avenue. Her father is very rich, and she is very fond of Mary."

"I should think she was—uncommonly," remarked Mrs. Carver.

"There's some secret here," she thought. "I must find it out."

"Mary, my dear," she said, aloud, "come here, and let me look at your pencil."

Mary advanced reluctantly. There was something in the visitor's tone that made her feel uncomfortable. It was evident that Mrs. Carver did not accept the account she had given as readily as her mother.

"It is a very handsome pencil," said Mrs. Carver, after examination. "You are certainly very lucky, Mary. My Grace is not so fortunate. So this Mrs. Cameron lives on Fifth Avenue?"

"Yes, ma'am."

"And her father sends her to a public school. That's rather singular,—isn't it?"

"So it is," said Mrs. Merton. "I didn't think of that. And the family is very proud too, you say, Mary?"

Mary by this time was quite willing to leave the subject, but Mrs. Carver was not disposed to do so.

"I don't know why it is," said Mary. "I suppose they think she will learn more at public schools."

"Now I think of it," said Mrs. Carver, meditatively, "this pencil looks very much like one I saw at Bennett's the other day."

The color rushed to Mary's face in alarm. Her mother did not observe it, but Mrs. Carver did. But she quickly recovered herself.

"Perhaps it was bought there,—I don't know," she said.

"She carries it off well," thought Mrs. Carver. "Never mind, I'll find out some time."

Mary made some excuse for leaving the room, and the visitor asked:—

"How is that girl getting along whom your brother left with you?"

Mrs. Merton shook her head.

"She's turned out badly," she said.

"What has she done?"

"She stole twenty dollars from Mr. Holland's room. He left his pocket-book on the bureau, and she took out the money."

"Did she confess it?"

"No, she stoutly denied it. I told her, if she would confess, I would forgive her, and let her stay in the house. But she remained obstinate, and went away."

"Are you convinced that she took it?" asked Mrs. Carver, who now suspected where the gold pencil came from.

"It could have been no one else. She was in the room, making the beds, and sweeping, in the morning."

"Still, she may have been innocent."

"Then who could have taken the money?"

"Somebody that wanted a gold pencil," returned Mrs. Carver, nodding significantly.

"What!" exclaimed Mrs. Merton, aghast. "You don't mean to hint that Mary took it?"

"I mean this, that she bought the pencil herself at Bennett's, as I happen to know. Where she got the money from, you can tell better than I can."

"I can't believe it," said Mrs. Merton, very much perturbed.

"Didn't you see how she flushed up when I said I had seen a pencil like it at Bennett's? However, you can ask her."

Mrs. Merton could not rest now till she had ascertained the truth. Mary was called, and, after an attempt at denial, finally made confession in a flood of tears.

"How could you let me send Jane away on account of your fault?" asked her mother, much disturbed.

"I didn't dare to own it. You won't tell, mother?"

"I must return the money to Mr. Holland."

"You can tell him that it was accidentally found."

This Mrs. Merton finally agreed to do, not wishing to expose her own child. She was really a kind-hearted woman, and was very sorry for her injustice to Tom.

"What will your uncle say?" she inquired, after Mrs. Carver had gone.

"Don't tell him," said Mary. "It's better for Jane to go, or he would be making her his heiress. Now I shall stand some chance. You can tell him that Jane went away of her own accord."

Mrs. Merton was human. She thought it only fair that one of her daughters should inherit their uncle's money in preference to a girl taken from the streets, and silently acquiesced. So the money was restored to Mr. Holland, and he was led to think that Tom had left it behind her, while the real perpetrator of the theft retained her gold pencil, and escaped exposure.

CHAPTER XVIII
IN SEARCH OF A PLACE.

Tom went out into the street angry, and justly so, at the unfounded charge which had been made against her. The change in her circumstances had been so sudden, that she hardly realized, as she walked along, that she must return to her old street life. When she did realize it, it was with a feeling of disappointment, not unmixed with apprehension.

Tom had only been living at Mrs. Merton's for three months, but this short time had wrought a considerable change in her. She was no longer the wild, untamed girl who once swept the crossing. She had begun to feel the advantages of respectability, and had become ambitious of acquiring a good education. This feeling originated in the desire of surprising Captain Barnes with her improvement; but she soon began to feel an interest in learning for its own sake. She was still spirited and independent, but in a different way. Her old life looked far less attractive, since she had acquired such different tastes. Now to be suddenly thrust back into it seemed rather hard to Tom.

One thing at least could be said, she was no longer "Tattered Tom." Her old rags had been cast aside, and she was now dressed as well as most school-girls. She no longer looked like a child having no home but the street, but would be supposed by any who noticed her to belong to some family in good circumstances. Now, good clothes exert more influence upon the wearer than we may at first suppose. So it was with Tom. When she wore her old tatters she was quite ready to engage in a fight with any boy who jeered at her, provided he was not too large. Now she would hesitate before doing it, having an undefined idea that her respectable dress would make such a scene unbecoming.

There was one question that presented itself to Tom as she walked along, and demanded her earnest attention. This was, "How was she to live?"

She could no longer sweep the crossing; she was too well-dressed for that. Indeed she was likely to attract attention if she engaged in any of the street occupations to which she had in former times been accustomed. But something must be done. Her whole stock of money consisted of five cents, and this was not likely to last very long. It was far too little to buy such a meal as she got at Mrs. Merton's. It was doubtful, Tom reflected with a sigh, when she would get another square meal.

Suddenly the thought came to Tom, could she not hire out to do chamber-work? She had learned to do this at Mrs. Merton's. It would be a great deal better than sweeping the crossing, or selling papers.

Tom did not know how such situations were obtained, but it occurred to her that she could go from one house to another, and apply.

With this plan in her mind, she turned round, and walked up town again. When she reached Twenty-First Street she decided to try her luck. Accordingly she went up to the front door of a handsome house with a brown stone front, and rang the bell.

The door was opened by a servant, who waited respectfully for her to announce her errand, supposing her to be a school-mate of one of the children of the family. Her neat dress favored this mistake.

"Is the lady of the house at home?" inquired Tom.

"Who shall I say wishes to see her?" asked the servant, doubtfully.

"Does she want to hire a girl to do chamber-work?" continued Tom.

"Who wants the place?"

"I do," said Tom.

"Then, she don't want any," said the girl, preparing to shut the door, with an entire change of manner. "Don't you know better than to come to the front door? There's the basement door below."

"One door's as good as another," said Tom, independently.

"Both are too good for you," said the servant, angry that under the influence of a mistake she had at first treated Tom with the respect due to a visitor.

"How much are you paid extra for your politeness?" asked Tom.

"Never you mind! You needn't call again."

Such was the result of Tom's first application. However, she was not discouraged. She reflected that there were a good many streets in the city, and a good many houses in each street. So she walked on, and rang the bell at the next house. She concluded to take the hint which had excited her indignation, and rang the basement bell.

"Do you want a girl to do chamber-work?" she asked.

Now it so happened that a chamber-maid was wanted here, and an order had been sent to an intelligence office for one. It was naturally supposed that Tom had come in answer to the application.

"Come in," said the servant. "I'll tell the missis that you are here."

She went upstairs, and shortly reappeared.

"You're to come up," she said.

Tom followed her upstairs, and took a seat in the hall.

Soon a lady came downstairs, with a languid step.

"Are you the girl that has applied to do chamberwork?" she said.

"Yes, ma'am," answered Tom.

"You seem very young. How old are you?"

"Twelve," answered Tom.

"Only twelve? I am surprised that so young a girl should have been sent to me. Have you any experience?"

"Yes, ma'am."

"Where have you lived?"

"At Mrs. Merton's, No. — Sixteenth Street."

"How long were you there?"

"Three months."

"Have you a recommendation from her?"

"No," answered Tom.

"Why did you leave?" asked the lady, suspiciously.

"Because she said I took some money, when I didn't," replied Tom, promptly.

A change came over the lady's face,—a change that betokened little encouragement to Tom.

"I shall not be able to take you," she said. "I wonder they should have sent you from the intelligence office."

"They didn't send me."

"You were not sent from the office? How did you know I wanted a chambermaid?"

"I didn't know," said Tom. "I thought you might."

"If I had known that, I should have refused you at once. You can go downstairs, and the servants will let you out at the basement door,—down those stairs."

"All right," said Tom. "I can find the way; you needn't come with me."

This last remark led the lady to stare at Tom, uncertain whether she meant to be impudent or not. But Tom looked so unconscious of having said anything out of the way that she passed it over in silence.

Tom made two more applications, which proved equally unsuccessful. She began to think it would be more difficult to obtain a situation than she had supposed. At any rate, she resolved to defer further applications till the morrow. Something might turn up then, she reflected with something of her old philosophy.

CHAPTER XIX
THE OLD APPLE-WOMAN.

When Tom had got through her unsuccessful applications for a place, it was already nearly five o'clock. She started on her way down town. Her old street life had been spent in the neighborhood of the City Hall Park. The offices of the leading daily and weekly papers may be found within a radius of a furlong from it. It is within this limit that hundreds of homeless young Arabs swarm, and struggle for a precarious living. In returning to her old life, Tom was drawn, as by a magnet, to this centre.

She walked down Fourth Avenue, and afterwards down the Bowery. It was three months since she had been in this street, which had once been so familiar to her. As she drew near the scene of her old life, she began to see familiar faces. She passed boot-blacks and newsboys whom she had once known and still remembered; but none of them appeared to recognize her. This surprised Tom at first, until she remembered what a change there was in her dress. Neatly dressed, she looked very different from the Tom who had roamed the streets in rags and tatters. She seemed to have cut adrift from her former life and from the sympathies of her old companions. This was not a pleasant thought, since she must now go back to it. Poor Tom began to regret that she had experienced anything better, since it seemed doubtful whether she would ever again be satisfied with a street life.

She did not make herself known to any of her old acquaintances, but walked slowly along till she reached the City Hall Park. She entered the inclosure and sat down on a seat. By this time she felt hungry as well as tired. She therefore purchased, before sitting down, two apples for three cents, thus diminishing her cash capital to two. The apples were large, and satisfied her appetite tolerably well. Still it was not like the dinner she would have got at Mrs. Merton's.

Supper was provided, but it would soon be night, and she must lodge somewhere. Tom had more than once slept out, like hundreds of other street children, and not minded it; but now, after being accustomed to a good chamber and a comfortable bed, she did not feel like doing this. Besides, her clothes would be spoiled, and Tom wanted to look respectable as long as she could.

She might go back to granny, but had no disposition to do that. Whatever she might be called upon to suffer, she felt that she should be better off alone than in the power of the bad old woman who had so maltreated her.

"I wish I could earn a few pennies," said Tom to herself. "I might buy some papers if I only had money enough."

While she was thinking, a boot-black had been surveying her curiously. It was Mike Murphy, an old acquaintance of Tom's. He thought he recognized her face, but her dress puzzled him. Where could Tattered Tom have procured such a stunning outfit? That was the mystery, and it made him uncertain of her identity. However, the face looked so familiar that he determined to speak.

"Is that you, Tom?" he asked.

Tom looked up, and recognised Mike at once. It seemed good to speak to an old acquaintance.

"Yes, Mike, it's me," said Tom, whose grammar was not yet quite faultless.

"Where'd you get them clo'es? You aint going to be married, be you?"

"Not that I know of," said Tom.

"Where've you been this long time? I haven't seen you round anywhere."

"I've been livin' up in Sixteenth Street," said Tom. "A sailor-man took me to his sister's, and got her to keep me."

"Did you like it?"

"Yes," said Tom. "I had three square meals every day. I went to school too."

"Did he buy you them clo'es?"

"Yes."

"Are you there now?"

"No, I left to-day."

"What for?"

"The old woman said I stole some money, and told me I must give it back or leave the house."

"How much did you steal?" asked Mike.

"Look here, Mike Murphy," said Tom, indignantly, "don't you say that again!"

"Didn't you take anything then?"

"Of course I didn't."

"What made her think so?"

"I don't know. Somebody took it, I s'pose, and she thought it was me."

"So you had to leave?"

"Yes."

"What are you goin' to do now?"

"I don't know," said Tom. "I haven't got but two cents, and I don't know where to sleep."

"Where's the old woman you used to live with?"

"I shan't go back to her," said Tom, firmly. "I hate her."

"You've got some good clo'es," said Mike. "I didn't know you, at first. I thought you was a young lady."

"Did you?" asked Tom, rather pleased.

The time had been when she did not want to look like a young lady,—when she would have preferred to be a boy. But her tastes had changed considerably since then. Something of the instinct of her sex had sprung up in her, as she was brought to a closer knowledge of more refined ways of life. She was no longer a young Arab in her feelings, as before. Three months had wrought a great change in Tom.

"If you haven't any place to sleep, Tom," said Mike, "you can come along of me."

"Can I?" asked Tom. "What'll your mother say?"

"Oh, she won't mind. Only you'll maybe have to sleep on the floor."

"I don't mind," said Tom. "It'll be better than sleeping in the street. Where do you live?"

"In Mulberry Street."

"I guess I'll get something to do to-morrow," said Tom.

"What did you use to do?"

"Sweep the crossings sometimes. I won't do that again. It's too dirty."

"It would sp'ile them nice clo'es of yours."

"Yes," said Tom. "Besides, I wouldn't want Mrs. Merton, or Mary, to see me doin' that."

"Who's Mary?"

"It's her child."

"Did you like her?"

"No, I didn't. She hated me too."

"Well, I'm goin' home. Come along, Tom."

Tom got up from her seat with alacrity, and prepared to accompany Mike. It was a great burden off her mind to think she was likely to have a shelter for the night. Perhaps something would turn up for her the next day. This thought brought back some of her old courage and confidence.

Mike Murphy's home was neither elegant nor spacious. Mulberry Street is not an aristocratic locality, and its residents do not in general move in fashionable society. Mrs. Murphy was a retail merchant, being the proprietor of an apple-stand on Nassau, near Spruce Street. Several years' exposure to the weather had made her face nearly as red as the apples she dealt in, and a sedentary life had enlarged her proportions till she weighed close upon two hundred pounds. In nearly all weathers she was to be found at her post, sometimes sheltered by a huge cotton umbrella, whose original color had been changed by the sun to a pale brown. Though she had not yet been able to retire from trade upon a competence, she had earned enough, with Mike's assistance, to support a family of six children,—in Mulberry Street style, to be sure, but they had never been obliged to go to bed hungry, and the younger children had been kept at the public school.

When Mike entered, his mother was already at home. She usually closed up her business about five o'clock, and went home to get supper.

She looked up as Mike entered, and regarded his companion with some surprise.

"What young leddy have you got with you, Mike?" asked Mrs. Murphy.

"She thinks you are a young lady, Tom," said Mike, laughing.

"Don't you know me, Mrs. Murphy?" asked Tom, who had known Mike's mother for several years.

"By the powers, if it aint Tom. Shure and you've had a rise in the world, I'm thinkin'. Why, you're dressed like a princess!"

"Maybe I am," said Tom; "but if I was one I'd be richer'n I am now."

"Tom was took up by a lady," explained Mike; "but she's sent her away, and she's got nothing barrin' her clo'es. I told her you'd let her sleep here to-night, mother."

"To be sure I will," said the kind-hearted woman. "It isn't much of a bed I can offer you, Tom, but it's better than sleepin' out."

"I can lie on the floor," said Tom. "I don't mind that."

"But why did the leddy turn you out?" inquired the apple-merchant.

Tom told her story, which Mrs. Murphy never thought of doubting.

"She's a hard, cruel woman. I'll say that for her, Tom dear," said Mrs. Murphy. "But never you mind. You're welcome to stay here, though it's a poor place. We're going to have some supper directly, and you must take some with us."

"I've eaten supper," said Tom.

"What did you have?"

"Two apples."

"I don't say nothin' ag'in' apples, for it's them I live by, but tay and toast is better for supper. Biddy, toast the bread, and I'll set the table. When a body's tired, a cup of tay goes to the right spot, and you'll find it so, Tom dear."

The good-hearted woman bustled about, and set the table, while Biddy, a girl of ten, toasted a large number of slices of bread, for the young Murphys were all blessed with good appetites. The tea soon diffused a fragrant aroma about the little room. Mrs. Murphy, humble as were her means, indulged in one solitary extravagance. She always purchased the best quality of "tay," as she called it, no matter what might be the price.

"It's a dale chaper than whiskey," she used to say, in extenuation of her extravagance. "It's mate and drink to me both, and warms me up besides, when I've got chilled by rason of stayin' out all day."

There was a plate of cold meat placed on the table. This, with the tea and toast, constituted Mrs. Murphy's evening repast.

"You can sit by me, Tom dear," she said, her face beaming with hospitality. "It isn't much I've got, but you are heartily welcome to what there is. Children, set up to the table, all of you. Mike, see that Tom has enough to ate. There's one thing I can give you, and that's a cup of illigant tay, that a quane might not turn up her nose at."

In spite of the two apples, Tom made room for a fair share of Mrs. Murphy's supper. Once more she felt that she had a home, humble enough, to be sure, but made attractive by kindness.

"I wish I could stay here," thought Tom; and it occurred to her that she might be able to make such an arrangement with the old apple-woman, on condition of paying a certain sum towards the family expenses.

CHAPTER XX
TOM SPECULATES IN GOLD.

During the evening some of the neighbors came in, and received a hearty greeting from Mrs. Murphy.

"And who is this young leddy?" asked Mrs. O'Brien, looking at Tom.

"It's a friend of mine," said Mrs. Murphy.

"Don't you know me?" asked Tom, who, in the days of her rags and tatters, had known Mrs. O'Brien.

"Shure and it isn't Tom?" said Mrs. O'Brien, in surprise.

"Did ye iver see such a change?" said Mrs. Murphy. "Shure and I didn't know her meself when she came in wid my Mike."

"It's mighty fine you're dressed, Tom," said Mrs. O'Brien. "Your granny aint come into a fortun', has she?"

"I don't live with granny now," answered Tom. "She's a bad old woman, and she isn't my granny either."

"It was only yesterday I saw her, and fine she was dressed too, wid a nice shawl to her back, and quite the leddy, barrin' a red nose. She says she's come into some money."

Tom opened wide her eyes in astonishment. She had speculated more than once on granny's circumstances, but it had never entered her thoughts that she had taken a step upwards in respectability.

"Where did you see her?" asked Tom.

"She was gettin' out of a Third Avenue car. She said she had just come from up town."

"She was lookin' after me, it's likely," said Tom.

"Where did she get her new clothes from?" Tom wondered.

"Maybe she's been adopted by a rich family in Fifth Avenoo," remarked Mike,—a sally which nearly convulsed his mother with laughter.

"Shure, Mike, and you'll be the death of me some time," she said.

"She'd make an interestin' young orphan," continued Mike.

"Hadn't you better marry her, Mike? and then you'd be my grandfather," suggested Tom.

"Such a beauty aint for the likes of me," answered Mike. "Besides, mother wouldn't want her for a daughter-in-law. She'd likely get jealous of her good looks."

"O Mike, you're a case!" said Mrs. Murphy, with a smile on her broad, good-humored face.

So the evening passed, enlivened with remarks, not very intellectual or refined, it is true, but good-natured, and at times droll. Tom enjoyed it. She had a home-feeling, which she had never had at Mrs. Merton's; and above all she was cheered by the thought that she was welcome, though the home was humble enough.

By and by the callers departed, and the family made preparations for bed.

"I can't give you a very nice bed, Tom," said Mrs. Murphy, "but I'll fix you up a place to slape on the floor wid my Biddy."

"That'll be jolly," said Tom. "If it wasn't for you, I'd have to sleep out in the street."

"That would be a pity, entirely, as long as I have a roof over me. There's room enough for you, Tom, and it won't be robbin' any of us."

Tom slept comfortably. Her bed was not one of the softest; but she had never been used to beds of down, sleeping on a hard straw bed even at Mrs. Merton's. She woke, feeling refreshed, and in much better spirits than when she set out from Mrs. Merton's.

When breakfast was over, Mrs. Murphy set out for her place of business, and Mike for his daily occupation. Biddy remained at home to take charge of the younger children. With the rest Tom went too.

"Come back to-night, Tom," said Mrs. Murphy.

"I should like to," said Tom, "if you'll let me pay for my board."

"Shure we won't quarrel about that. And what are you goin' to do, Tom, the day?"

"I don't know," said Tom. "If I had any money I'd buy some papers."

"How much wud you want?"

"Twenty-five cents would give me a start."

Mrs. Murphy dived into the recesses of a capacious pocket, and drew out a handful of currency.

"I'll lind it to you," she said. "Why didn't you ask me before?"

"Thank you," said Tom. "I'll bring it back to-night. You're very kind to me, Mrs. Murphy," she added, gratefully.

"It's the poor that knows how to feel for the poor," said the apple-woman. "It's I that'll trust you, Tom, dear."

Three months before Tom would have told Mrs. Murphy that she was a trump; but though some of her street phrases clung to her, she was beginning to use less of the slang which she had picked up during her long apprenticeship to a street life. Though her position, even at Mrs. Merton's, had not been as favorable as it might have been elsewhere, the influences were far better than in the home (if it deserved the name) in which she had been reared, and the association of the school which she attended had, likewise, been of advantage to her. I do not wish it to be understood that Tom had in three months changed from a young Arab into a refined young lady. That would be hardly possible; but she had begun to change, and she could never again be quite the wild, reckless girl whose acquaintance we made at the street-crossing.

Tom went out with Mrs. Murphy, helping her to carry her basket of apples. Leaving her at her accustomed stand, she went to the newspaper offices, and laid in a small supply. With these she went to Fulton Ferry, partly because she fancied that there was no danger of granny's coming there in pursuit of her. Even if the encounter did take place she was resolved not to go back. Still it was better to avoid it altogether.

Tom was rather late in the field. Most of her competitors had been selling papers for an hour, and some had already sold quite a number. However, not being in the least bashful, she managed to obtain her share of the trade that remained. The boats came in at frequent intervals, loaded down with passengers,—clerks, shop-boys, merchants, bankers, book-keepers, operatives, who made a home in Brooklyn, but spent the day in the busy metropolis.

"Morning papers, sir?" asked Tom, to a rather portly gentleman, who did business in Wall Street.

"Yes; give me the 'Herald.'"

He drew a coin from his pocket, and handed to Tom.

"Never mind about the change," he said.

Tom was about to put it in her pocket, supposing from the size that it was a five-cent piece; but, chancing to glance at it more particularly, she saw that it was a five-dollar gold piece.

Her eyes sparkled with joy. To her it was an immense fortune. She had never, in all her life, had so much money before. "But did he mean to give her so much?" was the question that suggested itself to her immediately. He had, to be sure, told her to keep the change, but Tom knew too much of human nature and the ways of the world to think it likely that anybody would pay five dollars in gold for a morning paper, without asking for a return of the change.

Now I am quite aware that in three cases out of four the lucky news-vender would have profited by the mistake, and never thought of offering to correct it. Indeed, I am inclined to think that Tom herself would have done the same three months before. Even now she was strongly tempted to do so. But she remembered the false charge that had been made against her by Mrs. Merton the day before, and the indignation she felt.

"If I keep this, and it's ever found out, she'll be sure I took the twenty dollars," thought Tom. "I won't do it. I won't let her call me a thief. I'll give it back."

The purchaser of the paper was already half through Fulton Market before Tom made up her mind to return the money. She started on a run, afraid her resolution might give way if she stopped to consider.

98

She easily recognized the man who had paid her the money.

"Mister," said Tom, touching him to attract his attention.

"What's wanted?" he inquired, looking at our heroine.

"Did you mean to give me this?" and Tom displayed the gold piece.

"Did I give it to you?"

"Yes, you bought a 'Herald,' you know, and told me to keep the change."

"Well, why didn't you?" he asked, in some curiosity.

"I thought you made a mistake."

"I shouldn't have found it out. Didn't you want to keep it?"

"Yes," said Tom, unhesitatingly.

"Why didn't you?"

"I thought it would be stealing."

"You're a natural phenomenon!"

"Is that a bad name?" demanded Tom.

"No, not in this case. So I told you to keep the change, did I?"

"Yes, sir."

"Then you'd better do it."

"Do you mean it?" asked Tom, astonished.

"To be sure. I never break my word."

"Then I'll do it," said Tom. "Aint I in luck this morning, though?"

"Yes, I think you are. As I probably know more of business than you, my young friend, will you permit me to give you a piece of advice?"

"All right," said Tom.

"Then, as gold is at a premium, you had better sell that gold piece, and take the value in currency."

"Where can I sell it?" asked Tom.

"I don't, in general, solicit business, but, if you have confidence in my integrity, you may call at my office, No. — Wall Street, any time to-day, and I will give you the market value of the gold."

"I don't understand all them big words," said Tom, rather puzzled, "but I'll go as soon as I have sold my papers."

"Very good. You may ask for Mr. Dunbar. Can you remember the name?"

Tom said she could, repeating it two or three times, to become familiar with it.

An hour later she entered the broker's office, looking about her for her acquaintance of the morning.

"Ah, there you are," said the broker, recognizing her.

"So you want to sell your gold?"

"Yes, sir."

"Gold sells at to-day. Will that be satisfactory?"

"Yes, sir."

"Mr. Johnson," said Mr. Dunbar, addressing a clerk, "give that young lady value in currency for five dollars in gold."

Tom handed in the gold, and received in return seven dollars and five cents. She could hardly credit her good luck, not being familiar with the mysteries of banking.

"Thank you, sir," said she gratefully, to the broker.

"I hope you will favor us with any future business you may have in our line," said Mr. Dunbar, with a friendly smile.

"Yes, sir," answered Tom, rather mystified by his manner, but mentally deciding that he was one of the jolliest gentlemen she had ever met.

When Tom emerged from the office, and was once more in the hurry and bustle of Wall Street, it is very doubtful whether, in that street of millionnaires and men striving to become such, there was a single one who felt so fabulously wealthy as she.

CHAPTER XXI

TOM FALLS INTO THE ENEMY'S HANDS.

Tom found herself the possessor of seven dollars and fifty cents, including the quarter which she owed to Mrs. Murphy for money advanced. It was not yet eleven o'clock. She decided to call on Mrs. Murphy, pay back the loan, and inform her of her good luck.

Mrs. Murphy was seated at her stand, keeping a sharp lookout for customers, when she espied Tom approaching.

"Have you sold your papers, Tom?" she asked.

"Yes, Mrs. Murphy. Here's the money I borrowed of you."

"Keep it longer; you'll maybe nade it. I aint afraid to trust you."

"I don't need it. I have been lucky. See there!" and Tom displayed a roll of bills.

"Where'd ye get all them?" asked the apple-woman, in amazement.

"A gentleman paid me a gold piece for a 'Herald,' and wouldn't take any change."

"Is it truth you're tellin', Tom?"

"Of course it is. Do you think I'd tell you a lie?"

"Tell me all about it, Tom."

Tom did so, to the intense interest of Mrs. Murphy, who, after ejaculations as to Tom's luck, added, "I wish he'd buy some apples of me, and trate me in the same way. And what are you goin' to do wid your money, Tom, dear?"

"I'm going to get a square meal pretty soon, Mrs. Murphy. If you'll come along, I'll treat you."

"Thank you, Tom, all the same, but I can't lave my business. You'd better put it in the savings-bank, where it'll be safe. Maybe you might lose it."

"Have you got any money in the savings-bank?"

"No, Tom, dear. It takes all I earn for the rint, and atin' for the childers."

"I want to live with you, Mrs. Murphy, if you'll take me."

"Shure and I'd be glad to have you, Tom, if you'll put up wid my poor room."

"I'd rather be there than at Mrs. Merton's," said Tom.

After some negotiation, Mrs. Murphy agreed to take Tom as a boarder, furnishing her with lodging, breakfast and supper, for a dollar and a half a week. It seemed a small sum, but it would be a welcome addition to the apple-woman's weekly income, while it would take Tom from the streets, and give her a cheerful and social home.

"I'll pay you now for a week," said Tom. "Then I'll be all right even if I lose the money."

After some persuasion, Mrs. Murphy was induced to accept the payment in advance.

"Now I'll go and get some dinner," said Tom.

Tom directed her steps to the Belmont House Restaurant, on Fulton Street. It has two rooms,—one for ladies, the other for gentlemen; and is well-patronized by a very respectable class, chiefly clerks and business men. It was of a higher grade than the restaurants which those in Tom's line of business were accustomed to frequent. Her dress, however, prevented any surprise being felt at her entrance. She sat down at a table, and looked over a bill of fare. She observed that roast turkey was marked forty cents. This was rather a large price for one in her circumstances to pay. However, she had been in luck, and felt that she could afford an unusual outlay.

"Roast turkey and a cup of coffee!" ordered Tom, as the waiter approached the table.

"All right, miss," said that functionary.

Soon the turkey was set before her, with a small dish of cranberry sauce, and a plate of bread and butter. Two potatoes and the cup of coffee made up Tom's dinner. She surveyed it with satisfaction, and set to with an appetite.

"I should like to live this way every day," thought Tom; "but I can't afford it."

The waiter brought a check, and laid it beside her plate. It was marked cents.

Tom walked up to the desk near the door, and paid her bill in an independent manner, as if she were accustomed to dine there every day. In making the payment she had drawn out her whole stock of money, and still held it in her hand as she stood on the sidewalk outside. She little guessed the risk she ran in doing so, or that the enemy she most dreaded was close at hand. For just at the moment Tom stood with her face towards Broadway, granny turned the corner of Nassau and Fulton Streets, and bore down upon her, her eyes sparkling with joy and anticipated triumph. She was not alone. With her was a man of thirty-five, bold and reckless in expression, but otherwise with the dress and appearance of a gentleman.

"There's the gal now!" said granny, in excitement.

"Where?" said her companion, sharing her excitement.

"There, in front of that eating-house."

"The one with her back towards us?"

"Yes. Don't say a word, and I'll creep up and get hold of her."

Tom was about to put back her money in her pocket, when she felt her arm seized in a firm grasp. Turning in startled surprise, she met the triumphant glance of her old granny.

"Let me alone!" said Tom, fiercely, trying to snatch away her arm.

"I've got you, have I?" said granny. "I knowed I'd get hold of you at last, you young trollop! Come home with me, right off!"

"I won't go with you," said Tom, resolutely. "I don't want to have anything to do with you. You haven't got anything to do with me."

"Haven't I, I should like to know? Aint I your granny?"

"No, you aint."

"What do you mean by that?" demanded Mrs. Walsh, rather taken aback.

"You aint any relation of mine. I don't know where you got hold of me; but I won't own such an old drunkard for a granny."

"Come along!" said granny, fiercely. "You'll pay for this, miss."

"Help!" exclaimed Tom, finding that she was likely to be carried away against her will, at the same time struggling violently.

"What's the matter?" asked a gentleman, who had just come out of the restaurant.

"It's my grand-child, sir," said Mrs. Walsh, obsequiously. "She run away from me, and now she don't want to go back."

"She hasn't got anything to do with me," said Tom. "Help!"

This last exclamation was intended to attract the attention of a policeman who was approaching.

"What's the trouble?" he demanded, authoritatively.

Mrs. Walsh repeated her story.

"What is the child's name?" asked the policeman.

"Jane," answered the old woman, who was at first on the point of saying "Tom."

"How long has she lived with you?"

"Ever since she was born, till a few weeks ago."

"What do you say to this?" asked the officer.

"I did live with her; but she beat me, so I left her. She says she is my granny, but she isn't."

"Where do you live now?"

"With Mrs. Murphy, in Mulberry Street."

This intelligence rather astonished granny, who heard it for the first time.

"Is the child related to you?" asked the officer.

"She's my grandchild, but she's always been a wild, troublesome child. Many's the time I have kept awake all night thinkin' of her bad ways," said granny, virtuously. "It was only yesterday," she added, with a sudden thought suggested by the sight of the money which she had seen Tom counting, "that she came to my room, and stole some money. She's got it in her pocket now."

"Have you taken any money from your grandmother?" demanded the policeman.

"No, I haven't," said Tom, boldly.

"I saw her put it in her pocket," said granny.

"Show me what you have in your pocket."

"I've got some money," said Tom, feeling in rather a tight place; "but it was given me this morning by a gentleman at Fulton Ferry."

"Show it," said the officer, authoritatively.

Tom was reluctantly compelled to draw out the money she had left,—a little over five dollars. Granny's eyes sparkled as she saw it.

"It's the money I lost," said she. "Give it to me;" and she clutched Tom's hand.

"Not for Joe!" said Tom, emphatically. "It's mine, and I'll keep it."

"Will you make her give it up?" asked granny, appealing to the policeman. "It's some of my hard earnings, which that wicked girl took from me."

"That's a lie!" retorted Tom. "You never saw the money. There was a gentleman down to Fulton Ferry that give it to me this morning."

"That's a likely story," said granny, scornfully.

"If you don't believe it you can ask him. He's got an office on Wall Street, No. —, and his name is Mr. Dunbar. Take me round there, and see if he don't say so."

"Don't believe her," said granny. "She can lie as fast as she can talk."

"Ask Mrs. Murphy then. She keeps an apple-stand corner of Nassau and Spruce Streets."

"You are sure she took this money from you?" inquired the policeman.

"Yes," said Mrs. Walsh. "I put it in my drawer yesterday forenoon, and when I come to look for it it was gone. Mrs. Molloy, that lives on the next floor, told me she saw Tom, I mean Jane, come in about three o'clock, when I was out to work. It was then that she took it."

If granny had been dressed in her old fashion, she would have inspired less confidence; but it must be remembered that, through money advanced by the lawyer, she was now, in outward appearance, a very respectable old woman; and appearances go a considerable way. The officer was, therefore, disposed to believe her. If he had any doubt on the subject it was settled by the interference of Mr. Lindsay, who had hitherto kept aloof, but who now advanced, saying, "I know this woman, Mr. Officer, and I can assure you that her story is correct. The child has been wild and rebellious, and stolen money. But her grandmother does not wish to have her arrested, as she might rightfully do. She prefers to take her back, and do what she can to redeem her."

Mr. Lindsay was in outward appearance a gentleman. His manner was quiet, and calculated to inspire confidence.

"That is sufficient," said the officer, respectfully. "Hark you," he added, addressing Tom, "you had better go away quietly with your grandmother, or I shall advise her to give you in charge for theft."

Granny had conquered. Tom saw that further immediate resistance would be unavailing; without a word, therefore, she allowed herself to be led away, mentally resolving, however, that her stay with granny would be brief.

CHAPTER XXII
THE LAWYER AND HIS CLIENT.

Mr. Selwyn, the lawyer who has already been introduced to the reader, sat in his office with a pile of papers before him, when a knock was heard at the door. His clerk being absent, he arose and opened it. A lady stood before him.

"Will you enter, madam?" he said.

"Is this Mr. Selwyn?" she asked.

"That is my name, madam."

"My name will probably be familiar to you. I am Mrs. Lindsay."

"I am glad to see you, madam. Will you be seated?"

She sat down, and the lawyer regarded with interest the client whom he now saw for the first time. She was still young, less than forty probably, and, though her face bore the impress of sorrow, she was still beautiful.

"I suppose you have no news for me," she said.

"I am sorry to say that I have as yet no trace of the child. Margaret Walsh is on the lookout for her, and, as you have made it worth her while, I do not doubt that she will eventually find her for you."

"Do you think my child is still in the city?" asked Mrs. Lindsay, anxiously.

"I have no doubt of it. A child, bred as she has been, does not often leave the city voluntarily, unless in the case of those children who are from time to time carried away to homes in the West, through the agency of the Children's Aid Society."

"But may she not be of the number of these?"

"I thought it possible, and have accordingly inquired particularly of the officers of the society whether any child answering to her description has been under their charge, and I am assured that this is not the case. She is probably earning a living for herself somewhere in the streets, though we cannot tell in what way, or in what part of the city. Having run away from Mrs. Walsh, whom I suspect she did not like, she probably keeps out of the way, to avoid falling again into her hands."

"It is terrible to think that my dear child is compelled to wander about the streets homeless, and no doubt often suffering severe privations," said Mrs. Lindsay, with a sigh.

"Have good courage, madam," said the lawyer. "I am convinced that we shall find her very soon."

"I hope indeed that your anticipations may be realized," said the mother. "But I have not yet told you what brings me to New York at this time."

Mr. Selwyn bowed and assumed an air of attention.

"It is not pleasant," said Mrs. Lindsay, after a slight pause, "to speak ill of a relative; but I am obliged to tell you that the worst foe I have is my brother-in-law, a younger brother of my late husband. It was he who in the first place contrived the abduction of the child, and, though he witnessed my distress, he has never relented, though it was doubtless in his power, at any time, to restore her to me."

"How lately have you become aware of his connection with the affair?"

"Only a few months since. One day I opened a desk belonging to him, in search of an envelope, when I accidentally came upon a letter from Margaret Walsh, written some years since, giving an account of her arrival in New York with my dear child, and claiming from him a sum of money which it appears he had promised as a compensation for her services. This discovery astounded me. It was the first intimation I had of my brother-in-law's perfidy. He had always offered me such a delicate and unobtrusive sympathy, and appeared to share so sincerely in my sorrow, that I could scarcely believe the testimony of my senses. I read the letter three times before I could realize his treachery. Of course I did not make known to him the discovery I had made, but, calling on a lawyer, I asked him to recommend to me some trustworthy gentleman in his profession in this city. Your name was suggested, and I at once authorized him to communicate with you, and employ you in the matter."

"I trust I shall prove worthy of the recommendation," said the lawyer, inclining his head.

"There is one question which I should like to ask," he continued. "In what manner would your brother-in-law be likely to derive advantage from your child's disappearance?"

"My husband left a large property," said Mrs. Lindsay. "Half of this was bequeathed to me, the remaining half I was to hold in trust for my child. If, however, she should die before reaching her majority, my brother-in-law, Mr. James Lindsay, was to receive my child's portion."

"That constitutes a very powerful motive," said the lawyer. "The love of money is the root of all evil, you know."

"I do not like to suspect my brother-in-law of such baseness," said Mrs. Lindsay, "but I fear I must."

"How are his own means? Has he considerable property?"

"He had. Both my husband and himself inherited a large property; but I have reason to think that, at the time I speak of, he had lost large sums by gambling. He had passed two years abroad, and I heard from acquaintances, who met him there, that he played for high stakes at Baden Baden and other German gambling resorts, and lost very heavily. I suspect that he must have reduced his means very much in this way."

"You are probably correct, and this supplies what we lawyers always seek—the motive. I can quite understand that to a man so situated a hundred thousand dollars must have been a powerful temptation. I must ask you another question. Has Mr. James Lindsay derived any advantage from your child's property thus far?"

"He has, though it was legally decided that he could not come into absolute possession, since my child's death was not definitely ascertained; at least, until such time as, if living, she would have attained her majority, it was decreed that the income derived from the property should be paid to him, this payment to cease only in case of Jenny's restoration."

"And has this been done?"

"It has."

"Then Mr. James Lindsay has for the last six years received the income of a hundred thousand dollars."

Mrs. Lindsay inclined her head.

"And you never suspected his agency in the affair, in spite of all this?"

"Never. I knew James profited by my dear child's loss, but I was not prepared to suspect him of such baseness."

"I should have thought of it at once; but then we lawyers see so much of the bad side of human nature that we are prone to suspect evil."

"Then I should not wish to be a lawyer. It pains me to think ill of others."

"I respect you for the sentiment, madam, though in my profession I am compelled to repudiate it. May I inquire whether your brother-in-law yet suspects that you have discovered his complicity in the plot against your child?"

"It is that which brings me to see you to-day. I feel sure that in some way he has gained a knowledge of my secret, though I endeavored to conceal it from him."

"That is not surprising. He might accidentally have seen the advertisement for Margaret Walsh, which, under your directions, I inserted in the leading New York daily papers."

"He must have found out in this way."

"He will now doubtless do what he can to prevent your recovering possession of her."

"I fear he has already commenced. Three days since, he told me that he was about to go to Washington, and possibly further south for a few weeks. He added that, having much business to occupy him, he doubted if he should be able to write often. I supposed this to be true, until yesterday I heard that, instead of taking the cars to Baltimore, he had bought a ticket for New York. This attempt to deceive me convinces me that he has penetrated my secret."

"Do you know where he is staying in New York?"

"No, I do not. I only reached the city to-day, and came at once to your office to inform you of the new danger which menaced our cause."

"The information is important, Mrs. Lindsay," said the lawyer, thoughtfully. "I must endeavor to guard against his machinations. No doubt he will first try to find out Margaret Walsh, and when he has found her will seek to buy her over to his interest. From what I know of the woman, he will have no difficulty in succeeding."

"What can we do?" asked Mrs. Lindsay, anxiously.

"I don't care to bid against him, for, having such large interests at stake, he will take care to go as high as we. We must do what we can to keep them apart."

"Will that be possible?"

"We can at least try. I must have time to think what methods are to be used."

"When shall you see Margaret?"

"To-morrow, probably. That is the day on which she has been accustomed to come for her weekly allowance, and I must do her the justice to say that she has never yet failed to present herself punctually. You will remain in New York?"

"Yes," said Mrs. Lindsay. "In my present state of mind I could not be contented away from here."

"What will be your address?"

"I have not thought."

"Let me advise you not to stop at a hotel. Your arrival would in that way become known to Mr. James Lindsay, as it would probably be published in the 'Evening Express.'"

"Can you recommend me a good boarding-house, Mr. Selwyn?"

"I know an excellent one on West Twenty-Fifth Street, where you will have a fine room and every comfort. I will, if you desire it, give you a letter to Mrs. Thurston, with whom I once boarded myself."

"I shall feel much indebted to you, Mr. Selwyn, if you will do so."

The lawyer turned to his desk, and wrote a brief note, which he handed to his client. She took it, and rose from her seat, saying, "May I hope to see you this evening, Mr. Selwyn? I am sorry to trespass upon your time to such an extent, but you will appreciate a mother's anxiety."

"I can and I do," said the lawyer; "and you may rest assured that my best energies shall be devoted to your service."

Within two hours Mrs. Lindsay found herself installed in a handsome apartment at Mrs. Thurston's boarding-house.

"I shall feel better," she reflected, "now that I am in the city where my child in all probability is leading a life of poverty and privation. God grant that she may be restored to me, and that I may be able to make up to her the care of which she has so cruelly been deprived for six long years!"

CHAPTER XXIII
HOW GRANNY AND TOM BECAME SEPARATED.
It will be understood why Mr. Lindsay had visited New York, and opened communication with Margaret Walsh. The knowledge that his sister-in-law had discovered his agency in the disappearance of her child, and the fear that she might recover her, and so deprive him of the large property for which he had intrigued, alarmed him, and led him to exert himself to frustrate, if possible, his sister's plans.

Only two days after reaching the city, he had met Margaret in the street. He recognized her at once, and discovered without much difficulty the steps Mrs. Lindsay had this far taken. He at once offered Margaret double the reward if she would serve his interests; and granny consented, nothing loth. The first object was still to get possession of Tom. How that was effected has already been told. We will now resume our story where we left it at the end of the twenty-first chapter.

Tom walked quietly away with granny, feeling that there was no chance of immediate escape. She meant to bide her time, and break away as soon as she could. Mr. Lindsay walked on the other side of granny until they reached the Astor House.

"Stop here a minute," he said, "I will go in and inquire when the next train starts on the Erie Road."

The old woman did as directed. Tom could not help wondering how there should be an acquaintance between granny and a well-dressed gentleman like Mr. Lindsay. It seemed strange, yet there was an evident understanding between them.

Mr. Lindsay came out in less than five minutes.

"A train starts in an hour," he said. "We had better go to the depot at once."

Granny made some objection to the short notice, but he overruled it.

"It must be done," he said, decidedly. "It is the only safe way."

"I aint used to travellin'," said Margaret.

"You've got a tongue in your head," he said roughly. "All you've got to do is to inquire when you are in doubt. I will go to the depot with you, and buy your tickets."

Mrs. Walsh made no further objection, and they took their way to the depot.

"I wonder what's up," thought Tom.

They reached the depot and went into the reception-room. Mr. Lindsay went out, and returned shortly with two strips of tickets, which he gave to granny, explaining in what way they would be called for. He then took out a roll of bills, and gave her. Then ensued a whispered conversation, of which Tom only heard detached words, from which she was unable to gather a definite idea. Then they entered the cars, and Mr. Lindsay left them, with a last injunction, "Mind she don't escape."

"I'll take care," nodded granny.

Soon the cars were on their way. It was the first time within her remembrance that Tom had ridden in the cars, and she looked out of the window with great interest, enjoying the rapid motion and the changing views. At last, yielding to curiosity, she turned and addressed the old woman.

"Where are we goin', granny?"

"Never you mind!" said granny.

"But I do mind. Are we goin' far?"

"None of your business!"

"Who was that man that gave you money? Has he got anything to do with me?"

"No," said granny.

"Why did he give you money?"

"Because he's a relation of mine," said granny. "He's my nephew."

Tom was not in the least deceived. She knew that, if granny had a nephew, he would be a far different man from Mr. Lindsay. However, she had a curiosity to hear what granny would say, and continued asking questions.

"Then he's a relation of mine," said Tom.

"No he isn't," said granny, sharply.

"Why isn't he? Aint you my granny?"

Mrs. Walsh could not gainsay this argument. "He's a little of a relation to you," she said. "He's give me some money, so I can live with you out West. You won't have to sweep streets no longer."

The mystery seemed to deepen. What truth there might be in granny's representations Tom could not tell. One thing was clear, however. Relation or not, this man had given granny money, and would probably give her more. Probably, if Tom remained with her, she would not fare as hard as formerly; but this she did not intend to do. She had come to dislike granny, who, she felt instinctively, was not really her relation, and still cherished the intention of running away as soon as there was a good opportunity.

Meanwhile the cars sped on till seventy-five miles separated them from the city. Broad fields extended on either side the railway track. To Tom, who was a true child of the city, who had rarely seen green grass, since the round of her life had been spent within a short distance of City Hall Park, it seemed strange. She wondered how it would seem to live in the country, and rather thought she should not like it.

At length they came to a station where supper was to be obtained. Granny was hungry and rose with alacrity.

"Shall I go with you?" asked Tom.

"No," said Mrs. Walsh, "set right here. I'll go and buy something for you."

They were so far away from the city now that granny had no fear of Tom's escaping, particularly as she had no money.

Tom retained her seat, therefore, and granny entered the station-house, where some of her fellow-passengers were already hurrying down their suppers.

She stepped up to the counter, and soon was engaged in a similar way.

"Will you have a cup of coffee, ma'am?" inquired the waiter.

"Haven't you got some whiskey?" inquired the old woman.

"No, we don't keep it."

Granny looked disappointed. She was very fond of whiskey, and, having plenty of money, saw no reason why she should be deprived of her favorite beverage.

"Aint there any to be got near by?" she asked.

"There's a saloon a few rods up the road," was the reply.

"Could I find it easy?"

"Yes, there's a sign outside. It's a small one-story building. You can't miss it."

Mrs. Walsh hastily bought a couple of cakes for Tom, and hurried out of the building. There stood the cars, liable to start at any time. It was the part of prudence to get in, and granny hesitated. But the desire for a dram was strong within her, and she thought she could run over and get a glass, and be back in time. The train stopped ten minutes for refreshments, and she had not consumed more than five. The temptation proved too strong for her to resist.

She reached the saloon, and, entering, said, "Give me a glass of whiskey, quick. I'm going right off in the train."

The whiskey was poured out, and granny drank it with a sense of exquisite enjoyment.

"Give me another," she said.

Another was poured out, and she had half drunk it, when the whistle was heard. This recalled the old woman to the risk she incurred of being left by the train. Setting down the glass hastily, she was hurrying out of the saloon, when she was stopped by the bar-tender.

"You haven't paid for your drinks, ma'am," he said bluntly.

Granny saw the train just beginning to move.

"I can't stop," she said desperately. "I shall be left."

"That don't go down!" said the bar-tender, roughly; "you must pay for your drinks."

"I'll send it to you," said granny, trying to break away.

"That trick won't work," said the man, and he clutched the old woman by the arm.

"I've got a gal aboard," screamed granny, desperately, trying at the same time to break away.

"I don't care if you've got forty gals aboard, you must pay."

Mrs. Walsh drew a bill from her pocket, and, throwing it down, rushed for the train without waiting for the change. But too much time had already been lost. The cars were now speeding along at a rate which made it quite impossible for her to catch them, and get aboard.

"Stop!" she shrieked frantically, running with a degree of speed of which she would have been thought incapable. "I've got a gal aboard. I shall lose her."

Some of the passengers saw her from the windows, and were inclined to laugh rather than sympathize with her evident distress.

"Serves her right!" said a grouty old fellow. "Why didn't she come back in time?"

"There's a woman left behind," said another passenger to the conductor.

He shrugged his shoulders, and said, indifferently, "That's her lookout. If she didn't choose to come to time, she must take the consequences."

"Couldn't you stop the train?" asked a kind-hearted little woman.

"No ma'am. Quite impossible. We're behind time already."

So the train sped on, leaving granny frantic and despairing, waving her arms and screaming hoarsely, "Stop! I've got a gal aboard!"

"What would Mr. Lindsay say?" she could not help thinking. Only four hours had passed since Tom had been placed in her charge, and they were separated. She cared little or nothing for Tom, or her welfare, but for her own interests, which were likely to be seriously affected, she cared a great deal. She was to have a comfortable annuity as long as she kept Tom safe in custody, and that was at an end unless she could manage to get her back.

She went into the station-house, and inquired when the next train would leave. She learned that several hours must elapse. Having plenty of time, therefore, she went back to the saloon, and recovered the change due her, taking an additional glass of whiskey, to drown her chagrin and disappointment.

CHAPTER XXIV
TOM'S ADVENTURES.

Among those who looked out of the window, and witnessed granny's frantic gesticulations was Tom.

"Aint that rich?" she uttered, in high delight.

"What's the matter?" asked an old lady, who sat just in front, bending over and speaking to Tom.

"It's my granny," said Tom, laughing afresh. "She's left behind. You ought to see her shakin' her fist at the cars."

"Are you laughing at your grandmother's disappointment?" asked the old lady's daughter, a prim-visaged maiden lady. "For shame, child!"

"I'm glad to get rid of her," said Tom, coolly. "She aint my granny; she only pretends to be."

"Hasn't she had the care of you?"

"No," said Tom. "I've had the care of her. She took all the money I earned, and spent it for rum."

"What are you going to do?" inquired the old maid.

"I don't know," said Tom, her attention being now first called to the embarrassment of her situation. She was nearly eighty miles from New York, and this distance was fast increasing. She had no railway ticket and no money. What was she to do?

"Have you had any supper, child?" asked the old lady.

"No," answered Tom. "Granny went out to get some."

"Priscilla," said the old lady, "haven't you got some of them cookies left?"

"Yes, ma," said the daughter.

"You'd better give some of them to the child."

The younger lady took several hard seed-cakes from a paper bag, and offered them to Tom, who accepted and ate them with avidity.

Meanwhile she was considering what was best to be done. She wanted to get back to New York, where she felt at home. Then she could go back to Mrs. Murphy's, whom she had paid for a week's board in advance. She had no money, for granny had forcibly taken from her what she had left after paying for her dinner. How she was to get back seemed rather a problem. One thing, however, appeared evident: every moment carried her farther away from the city. So Tom concluded that the sooner she got off, the better.

When the cars reached the next stopping-place, Tom got up and went to the door.

"Where are you going?" asked the old lady.

"I'm going to look out," answered Tom, fearing that some impediment might be placed in her way.

"Don't you get off, or you may get lost too."

"All right."

Tom stepped on the platform, and, quietly jumping from the cars, ran round the depot, to escape notice. The stop was a short one, and directly she heard the noise of the departing train. When it was fairly on the way, Tom began to look around her and consider her situation.

It was a small station, and there was scarcely a house near the depot. It was already twilight, and to Tom, who was accustomed to the crowded city, it appeared very lonely and desolate. She knew not where she should pass the night. She had often been in that position in the city, and it did not trouble her. Here, however, she was rather startled at the unwonted solitude. Besides, being wholly ignorant of the country, it occurred to her that she might meet some wild animal prowling around.

Just as this thought came into her mind, she saw advancing towards her a cow, followed by a farmer's boy, about two years older than herself. Now Tom was brave enough constitutionally, but this was the first cow she had ever seen, and the branching horns led her to suppose it fierce and dangerous, like a lion, for example.

She rushed with headlong speed to a stone wall and climbed over.

"Ho! ho!" laughed the boy; "are you afraid of a cow?"

"Won't she kill me?" asked Tom, a little reassured.

"She wouldn't kill a fly. Didn't you ever see a cow afore?"

"No, I didn't," said Tom. "I thought it was something like a lion."

"Where've you lived all your life?" asked the boy, astonished at Tom's greenness, as he considered it.

"In New York."

"I thought everybody'd seen cows. Where are you going?"

"I don't know," answered Tom.

"You aint stoppin' to Doctor Simpson's, be you?"

"I'm stoppin' on this fence," said Tom, rather humorously.

"Taint a fence; it's a stone wall."

"What's the odds?"

"How did you come here?"

"By the cars," said Tom. "I got left."

"You did? Where are you going to sleep to-night?"

"I don't know."

"There's a tavern in the village."

"What's that?"

"A tavern. Don't you know? A hotel."

"I haven't got any money."

"That's queer," said the boy, staring. "Where are you goin' to sleep?"

"On the grass," said Tom; "only I'm afraid of the wild animals."

"Pooh! there aint no wild animals round here. But you mustn't sleep out-doors. You'll catch cold. If you'll come home with me, mother'll let you sleep in our house."

"Thank you," said Tom. "You're a brick."

"You talk queer for a girl. What's your name?"

"Tom."

"Tom? That's a boy's name."

"They call me so. My right name is Jane."

"Well, Jane, come along, and I'll show you where we live."

The two walked together, soon becoming sociable. The boy, James Hooper, was amazed at Tom's ignorance of the most common things pertaining to country life, but found that in other ways she was sharp enough.

"You talk just like a boy," he said.

"Do I?" said Tom. "I used to wish I was a boy, but I don't know now. I think I'd like to grow up a lady,—a tip-top one, you know,—and dress fine."

"Are all the girls in New York like you?" asked James, curiously.

"No," said Tom. "There's Mary Merton, she isn't a bit like me. This is the way she walks," and Tom imitated Mary's languid, mincing gait.

"I like you best," said John. "But here we are. Do you see that house down the lane?"

"Yes," said Tom.

"That's where we live."

It was a large, square, comfortable farm-house, such as we often see in farming towns. The farmer's wife, a stout, comely woman, stood at the door.

"Who've you got with you, James?" she asked.

"It's a girl that got left by the train," said James. "She's got no money to pay for her lodging. I told her you would let her sleep here."

"Of course I will. Come right in, child. How did you get left?"

"I just got out a minute," said Tom, "and the cars went off and left me."

"What a pity! Who was travelling with you?"

"My granny," answered Tom.

"What'll she do? She'll be very much frightened."

"I expect she will," said Tom, who had made up her mind not to tell too much.

"Were you going back to the city?"

Tom answered in the affirmative. I do not mean to defend the lie, for a lie it was, but I have not represented Tom as perfect in any respect. In the future she will improve, I hope, when placed under more favorable circumstances. Her object in saying what she did was to prevent any opposition being made to her return to the city.

"You haven't had any supper, have you?" asked Mrs. Hooper.

"I ate a few cakes," answered Tom.

"That isn't hearty enough for a growing girl," said the good woman. "You must take some supper with us."

The family supper had been eaten, but a tempting array of dishes was soon set before Tom, whose appetite was always ready to answer any reasonable demands upon it.

In the evening Tom's best course was discussed. She expressed a strong desire to return at once to the city, saying she would be all right there.

"If your grandmother would not feel anxious about you," said Mrs. Hooper, "we should be glad to have you stop with us a day or two."

"I guess I'd better go back," said Tom, for, knowing that granny had been left by the cars only five miles away, she was under some apprehensions that she might find her way thither.

"You can take the nine-o'clock train to-morrow morning," said James, "and get to the city before night."

"Before night? She'll get there by one o'clock," said his mother.

"I haven't got any money to buy a ticket," said Tom.

"We will lend you the necessary amount," said the farmer, "and your grandmother can pay it back whenever it is convenient."

Tom felt a little reluctant to accept this money, for she knew that there was no hope of repayment by granny; but she determined to accept it, and work hard till she could herself save up money enough to pay the debt incurred. She felt grateful to the farmer's family for their kindness, and was resolved that they should not suffer by it.

In the evening they gathered in the plain sitting-room, covered with a rag-carpet. Tom helped James make a kite. She was ignorant, but learned readily. In her interest, she occasionally let slip some street phrases which rather surprised James, who was led to wonder whether Tom was a fair specimen of New York girls. He had always fancied that he should feel bashful in their society; but with Tom he felt perfectly at home.

In the morning he accompanied Tom to the depot, and paid for her ticket, being supplied with money for the purpose by his mother.

"Good-by," he said, shaking her hand as she entered the cars.

"Good-by, old fellow," said Tom. "I'll pay you back that money if granny don't."

The train started and was soon whirling along at the rate of twenty miles an hour. Half-way between this and the next station they passed a train bound in an opposite direction. Looking through the window on the side towards the other train, Tom caught a glimpse of granny's face. The old woman had been compelled to stop till morning, and had taken the first train bound westward. She did not see Tom, who quickly moved her head from the window.

"Sold again!" thought Tom, in high delight. "When granny catches me again, she'll know it."

CHAPTER XXV
TOM FINDS HER MOTHER.

Tom sat back in her seat and enjoyed the prospect from the windows, as the train sped along. She felt in unusually good spirits, knowing that she had put granny entirely off the track, and that there was no immediate chance of her recapture.

"If I only had that money granny took from me, I'd be all right," she said to herself. However, her board and lodging were paid at Mrs. Murphy's for a week in advance, and that was something.

About forty miles from New York a number of passengers got into the cars. The seats were mostly occupied, but the one beside Tom was untaken. A gentleman advanced up the aisle with a lady, looking about him for a seat.

"Is this seat engaged?" he inquired of Tom.

"No," answered Tom.

"Then you had better sit here, Rebecca," said the gentleman. "I think you will have no trouble. You won't forget where you are to go,—Mrs. Thurston's, West Twenty-Fifth Street. I can't recall the number, but a glance in the Directory will settle that."

"I wish you knew the number," said the lady.

"It was very careless of me to lose it, I confess. Still, I think you will have no trouble. But good-by, I must hurry out, or I shall be left."

"Good-by. Let me see you soon."

The gentleman got out, and the lady settled down into her seat, and looked about her. Finally her glance rested on her young companion. She was inclined to be social, and accordingly opened a conversation with Tom.

"Are you going to New York?" she inquired.

"Yes, ma'am."

"I suppose you live there?"

"Yes."

"I have never been there, and know nothing at all about the city."

"It's a big place," remarked Tom.

"Yes, I suppose so. I have always lived in the country, and I am afraid I shan't feel at home there. But my sister, who is boarding with a Mrs. Thurston, who keeps a large boarding-house on West Twenty-Fifth Street, has invited me to come up and spend a few weeks, and so I have got started."

"I guess you'll like it," said Tom.

"Do you live anywhere near West Twenty-Fifth Street?"

"Not now," said Tom. "I did live in West Sixteenth Street, but I don't now."

"Are you travelling alone?"

"Yes," said Tom.

"I suppose you live with your father and mother?"

"I haven't got any," answered Tom, laconically.

"I suppose you are well acquainted with the city?"

"Yes," said Tom. "I know it like a book."

The fact was, that Tom knew it a great deal better than a book, for her book-knowledge, as we very well know, was by no means extensive.

"Do you board?"

"Yes," said Tom. "I board with Mrs. Murphy, in Mulberry Street."

It struck the lady that Murphy was an Irish name, but the name of the street suggested nothing to her. She judged from Tom's appearance that she belonged to a family in comfortable circumstances.

"I wish I knew the number of Mrs. Thurston's house," said the lady rather anxiously. "I'm so afraid I shan't find it."

"I'll tell you what," said Tom, "I'll go with you, if you want me to."

"I wish you would," said the lady, much relieved. "It would be a great favor."

"I s'pose you won't mind givin' me a quarter," added Tom, with a sharp eye to the main chance; not unreasonably, since she was penniless.

"I'll give you double that amount," said the lady, "and thank you into the bargain. I'm not much used to travelling, and feel as helpless as a child."

"I'll take care of you," said Tom, confidently. "I'll take you to Mrs. Thurston's right side up with care."

"She talks rather singularly," thought the lady; but Tom's confident tone inspired her with corresponding confidence, and she enjoyed the rest of her journey much more than she would otherwise have done. Tom's request for compensation did not surprise her, for she reflected that children have always a use for money.

At length they reached the city, and Tom and her companion got out of the cars.

"Come right along," said Tom, taking the lady by the hand as if she were a child.

"Carriage, ma'am?" asked several hackmen.

"Perhaps I'd better take a carriage," said the lady, whose name, by the way, was Mrs. Parmenter.

"Just as you say," said Tom.

"I've got a nice carriage, ma'am. This way, please," said a burly driver.

"Look here, mister, what are you going to charge?" demanded Tom.

"Where do you want to go?"

"To Mrs. Thurston's, West Twenty-Fifth street."

"Whereabouts in the street? What number?"

"The lady don't know."

"Then how am I to carry you there?"

"Look into the Directory," said Tom. "If it's too much trouble for you, we'll take another man."

The hackman made no further objections, but resolved to increase his charge to compensate for the extra trouble. But here again Tom defeated him, compelling him to agree to a price considerably less than he at first demanded.

"Young lady," said he, paying an involuntary tribute to Tom's shrewdness, "you're about as sharp as they make 'em."

"That's so," said Tom. "You're right the first time."

Mrs. Parmenter and Tom entered the carriage, and the driver mounted his box.

"I don't see how you dared to talk to that man so," said the lady. "I should have paid him whatever he asked."

"Then you'd have got awfully cheated," said Tom. "I know their tricks."

"I'm sure I'm much obliged to you. I don't know how I should have got along without you."

"I've always lived in the city," said Tom; "so I've got my eye-teeth cut. They can't cheat me easy."

"I'm afraid I'm selfish in taking you with me," said Mrs. Parmenter. "I hope your friends won't be alarmed at your coming home late."

"I don't think they will," said Tom, laughing.

"You said you had no relatives living in the city?"

"Not now. My granny's just left New York. She's travellin' for her health," added Tom, with a burst of merriment, at which Mrs. Parmenter was rather surprised.

"Where has she gone?"

"Out West. I went a little way with her, just to oblige. She was awful sorry to part with me, granny was;" and Tom laughed again in a manner that quite puzzled her companion, who mentally decided that Tom was a very odd girl indeed.

"After we get to Mrs. Thurston's," said Mrs. Parmenter, "I'll tell the driver to carry you home. Shall I?"

Tom fancied the sensation she would produce in Mulberry Street, if she should drive up to the door of the humble tenement house in which she boarded, and declined the offer. She might have accepted, for the joke of it, but she saw that the hackman took her for a young lady, and she did not wish to let him discover the unfashionable locality in which she made her home.

"Never mind," said Tom. "I'd just as lieves ride in the cars."

They stopped at a drug-store, and the driver, going in, ascertained without difficulty, by an examination of the Directory, the number of Mrs. Thurston's boarding-house. A few minutes later, he drew up in front of a very good-looking house, and, jumping from the box, opened the door.

"Is this Mrs. Thurston's?" asked Mrs. Parmenter.

"Yes, ma'am; it's the number that's put down in the Directory."

"I'll ring the bell and see," said Tom.

She ran up the steps, and rang a loud peal, which was quickly answered.

"Is this Mrs. Thurston's?" she asked.

"Yes."

"Then here's a lady that's coming in," said Tom. "It's the right place," she added, going back to the carriage where Mrs. Parmenter was engaged in paying the driver.

"Now, my dear," said Mrs. Parmenter, "I hope you'll accept this for your kindness in guiding me."

She drew a dollar from her purse, and handed it to Tom.

"Thank you," said Tom, quite elated. "I'm glad I come with you."

Mrs. Parmenter was about to enter the house, when another lady descended the steps. It was Mrs. Lindsay, who had been recommended to this house, as the reader may remember, by the Wall Street lawyer. She no sooner saw Tom than she became excited, and grasped the balustrade for support.

"Child," she said, eagerly, "what is your name?"

"Tom," answered our heroine, surprised.

"Tom?"

"That's what they call me. Jane is my real name."

"Do you know a woman named Margaret Walsh?" continued Mrs. Lindsay, her emotion increasing.

"Why, that's my granny," said Tom, surprised.

There was no more room for doubt. Mrs. Lindsay opened her arms.

"Found at last!" she exclaimed. "My dear, dear child!"

"Are you my mother?" asked Tom, in amazement.

"Yes, Jenny, your own mother, never again, I hope, to be separated from you;" and Mrs. Lindsay clasped the astonished girl to her arms.

"You don't look a bit like granny," she said, scanning the refined and beautiful features of her mother.

"You mean Margaret," said Mrs. Lindsay, with a shudder. "She is a wicked woman. It was she who stole you away from me years ago."

"I played such a trick on her," said Tom, laughing. "She wanted to carry me off out West; but I left her, and she's goin' on alone."

"Come in, my darling," said Mrs. Lindsay. "Your home is with your mother henceforth. You have much to tell me. I want to know how you have passed all these years of cruel separation."

She took Tom up to her own chamber, and drew from her the whole story. Many parts gave her pain, as Tom recounted her privations and ill-treatment; but deep thankfulness came at the end, because the child so long-lost was at last restored.

"To-morrow I must buy you some new clothes," said she. "Are these all you have?"

"Yes," said Tom, "they are a good deal nicer than I used to wear."

"You shall have better still. I will try to make up to you for your past privations."

"I want to go out a little while," said Tom. "I'd like to tell Mrs. Murphy what's happened to me. You see, I paid her for a week's board, and she'll wonder where I am."

"I can't trust you out of my sight," said Mrs. Lindsay; "but I'll go with you if you wish it."

"Yes, I should like that."

Great was the astonishment of worthy Mrs. Murphy, when Tom came up to her stand with a handsomely dressed and stylish lady, whom she introduced as her mother. I will not attempt to repeat the ejaculations in which she indulged, nor her delight when Mrs. Lindsay bought one of her apples for Tom, and paid for it with a ten-dollar bill, refusing change.

"Shure, your mother's a rale leddy, Tom dear," she said; "and it's I that's glad of it, for your sake."

Mrs. Lindsay ordered dinner for herself and Tom in her own room, not wishing to introduce her to her fellow-boarders until she had supplied her with a more suitable wardrobe, for Tom's dress was by this time soiled and dirty. When the lawyer came up in the evening, his surprise was great to find the child, whom he had exhausted his legal skill to discover, already restored to her mother. He offered his sincere congratulations, and, it may here be remarked, was handsomely paid for the trouble he had taken in the matter.

By the next post, at Tom's request, a letter was sent by Mrs. Lindsay to the farmer's wife who had sheltered Tom, enclosing the amount of money paid for the railroad ticket, and thanking her earnestly for the kindness shown to her child. Much to Tom's delight, an extra ten dollars was enclosed as a present to James Hooper from her.

CHAPTER XXVI
CONCLUSION.

When Tom was suitably dressed, it was easy to perceive a strong resemblance between her mother and herself. This resemblance was affected, to be sure, by a careless, independent expression produced by the strange life she had led as a street Arab. No doubt her new life would soften and refine her manners, and make her more like girls of her own age.

Having no further occasion to remain in New York, Mrs. Lindsay took the train for Philadelphia the next day, where Tom, whom we must now call Jane Lindsay, found herself in an elegant home, surrounded by all that wealth could supply. Her mother lost no time in supplying her with teachers, that the defects of her education might be remedied. These were great, as we know, but Jane—I had nearly said Tom—was quick, and her ambition was excited, so that the progress which she made was indeed remarkable. At the end of the year she was as far advanced as most girls of her age.

At first our heroine found the change in her life not altogether agreeable. She missed the free life of the streets, which, in spite of all its privations and discomforts, is not without a charm to the homeless young Arabs that swarm about the streets. But in a short time she acquired new tastes, never, however, losing that fresh and buoyant spirit, and sturdy independence, which had enabled her to fight her way when she was compelled to do so. It was evident that Jane, whether from her natural tendencies or her past experiences, was not likely to settle down into one of those average, stereotyped, uninteresting young ladies that abound in our modern society. Nature was sure to assert itself in a certain piquancy and freshness of manner, which, added to her personal attraction, will, I think, eventually make Tom—the name slipped from my pen unintentionally—a great favorite in society. Her faults, at some of which I have hinted, she did not at once get rid of; but the influence of an excellent mother will, I am convinced, in time eradicate most of them.

When James Lindsay learned that his sister-in-law had recovered her child, he went abroad without seeing her, being ashamed no doubt to meet one whom he had so deeply injured, and there was no difficulty in reclaiming the property, the income of which had for some years been wrongly diverted to his use.

Such of my readers as have conceived an admiration for granny may be interested to learn that she kept on in her western journey, hoping to come upon Tom somewhere; but of course she was disappointed. She arrived at length in Chicago, and, having a considerable sum of money in her possession, decided to stay there. She did not venture to open communication with James Lindsay, lest he should take from her the money she had at present, on account of her careless guardianship. Hiring a room, she gave herself up to the delights of drinking and smoking. The last habit proved fatal, when, one afternoon, she lay down with her lighted pipe in her mouth. Falling asleep, the pipe fell upon the bed, setting on fire the bedclothes, and next the clothing of Margaret herself. Whether she was suffocated before awakening, or whether she awoke too late for rescue, was never ascertained. Certain it is, however, that when the smell of smoke called in the neighbors, granny was quite dead, expiating by her tragical end the sins of her miserable career.

I must sketch one more scene, and then this chronicle of Tom's adventurous life will close.

Fifteen months after Tom made the acquaintance of Captain Barnes, that worthy officer returned to New York. He at once repaired to the house of his sister, Mrs. Merton, expecting to find Tom. He had thought of her very often while at sea, and pictured with pleasure the improvement which she would exhibit after a year's training and education.

"I have no child. I probably shall never have one," he said to himself. "If Jenny has become such a girl as I hope, I will formally adopt her, and when I have become too old to go to sea, we will make a pleasant and cosey little home together, and she shall cheer my declining years."

Such thoughts as these warmed the heart of the sailor, and made him anxious for the voyage to close. He had heard nothing from his sister since he left, and was, therefore, ignorant of the fact that Tom was no longer in her charge.

When he reached his sister's house, and had kissed her and his nieces, he inquired eagerly:—

"Where's Jane? Has she improved?"

"Then you haven't heard, Albert," said his sister, not without embarrassment, for she was about to deceive him.

"Heard! What is there to hear?" he said impatiently.

"Jane has not been with me for a year."

"What has become of her?"

"Indeed I don't know. She remained with me three months after you left, and then suddenly disappeared. She must have got tired of a life so different from that she had been accustomed to lead, and determined to go back to her street life."

"I am deeply grieved to hear it," said Captain Barnes. "I have anticipated meeting her with so much pleasure. And have you never seen her since?"

"Never."

"I thought you might accidentally have met her in the street."

"No."

"Had she improved while she did stay?"

"Yes," said Mrs. Merton, with hesitation, "that is, a little. She was not quite so wild and rude as at first; but I don't think she would ever have made up the deficiencies of her early training."

Captain Barnes paced the floor, deeply disturbed. His disappointment was a great one.

"I shall try to trace her," he said at length. "I will apply to the police for help."

"That's the best thing to do, uncle," said Mary, with a sneer. "Very likely you'll find her at Blackwell's Island."

"For shame, niece," said her uncle, sternly. "You might have a little more charity for a poor girl who has not had your advantages."

Mary was abashed, and regretted that she had spoken so unguardedly, for she hoped to produce a favorable impression upon her uncle, in the hope of becoming his heiress.

The silence was broken by the stopping of a carriage before the door. Mary flew to the window.

"O mother," she said, "there's a beautiful carriage at the door, with a coachman in livery, and there's a lady and a young girl, elegantly dressed, getting out."

Quite a sensation was produced by the intelligence.

A moment later, and the servant brought in the cards of Mrs. Lindsay and Miss Lindsay.

"I don't remember the name," said Mrs. Merton, "but you may show the ladies in, Hannah."

Directly afterwards Mrs. Lindsay and our heroine entered the room. They were visiting friends in New York, and Jane had induced her mother to call at the house where she had learned her first lessons in civilization. She was very different now from the young Arab of fifteen months since. She was now a young lady in manners, and her handsome dress set off a face which had always been attractive. Neither Mrs. Merton nor Mary dreamed of associating this brilliant young lady with the girl whom they had driven from the house by a false charge.

"Good-morning, Mrs. Lindsay," said Mrs. Merton, deferentially. "Won't you and the young lady take seats?"

"You are no doubt surprised to see me," said Mrs. Lindsay, "but my daughter wished me to call. She was for three months, she tells me, a member of your family."

"Indeed," said Mrs. Merton, in surprise, "I think there must be some mistake. I don't remember that Miss Lindsay ever boarded with me."

"Don't you remember Tom?" asked Jane, looking up, and addressing Mrs. Merton in something of her old tone.

"Good gracious! You don't mean to say—" ejaculated the landlady, while Mary opened wide her eyes in astonishment and dismay.

"For years," explained Mrs. Lindsay, "my daughter was lost to me through the cruel schemes of one whom I deemed a faithful friend; but, thank God, she was restored to me within a week after she left your house."

"Was that the reason of your leaving, Jane?" asked Captain Barnes.

"Mother," said Jane, cordially grasping the hand of the captain, "this is the kind gentleman who first found me in the street, and provided me with a home."

"Accept a mother's gratitude," said Mrs. Lindsay, simply, but with deep feeling.

"I was sure you would turn out right, Jane," said the captain, his face glowing with pleasure. "Then you left my sister, because you found your mother?"

"No, that was not the reason," said Jane, looking significantly at Mrs. Merton, who, knowing that she had suspected her of what was really her daughter's fault, felt confused and embarrassed.

"There was a—a little misunderstanding," she stammered, "for which I hope Miss Lindsay will excuse me. I found out my mistake afterwards."

No further explanation was then given, but Captain Barnes required and obtained an explanation afterwards. He blamed his sister severely, and Mary even more, and that young lady's prospects of becoming her uncle's heiress are now very slender.

"I hope, Captain Barnes," said Mrs. Lindsay, "you will come to Philadelphia and pass a few days at my house. Nothing would please my daughter more, nor myself."

The good captain finally accepted this invitation, though with diffidence, and henceforth never arrived in port without visiting his former protegée, where he always found a warm welcome.

And so my story ends. My heroine is now a young lady, not at all like the "Tattered Tom" whose acquaintance we first made at the street-crossing. For her sake, her mother loses no opportunity of succoring those homeless waifs, who, like her own daughter, are exposed to the discomforts and privations of the street, and through her liberality and active benevolence more than one young Arab has been reclaimed, and is likely to fill a respectable place in society.

The next story of this series will be

PAUL, THE PEDDLER;
OR,
The Fortunes of a Young Street Merchant.

CPSIA information can be obtained
at www.ICGtesting.com
Printed in the USA
LVHW091326090122
708134LV00004B/334